RECON TEAM FOUR

"I've seen crazy," Jason said.

And Jason had. He had stood in the middle of a fight, firing his M-4, with bullets and tracers raining down on his position, but leaving him untouched. He had seen Joe hold an alley on his own, against what seemed like a small army, until they had fled.

Grimm was different, though, and Jason wanted to know why. "So just tell me."

Another long pause from the Ranger. Jason could sense him hanging on the edge. As if wanting to tell someone his secret. Like it was eating Grimm alive, and he knew that all he had to do was talk about it, and he could survive whatever it was.

But Grimm still kept quiet. A minute passed. Another.

"All I'll say," Grimm finally said, "is something dark is down there. I'm pretty sure I've seen bad things. This thing, it's different. Bigger. Worse."

"But you don't know what it is?" Jason pressed.

Grimm shook his head. "No."

"But you know it's there?" Jason asked.

Grimm nodded once. "I do."

BOOKS BY CHRIS J. CRANFORD

RECON TEAM FOUR

A Grimm Story

CHRIS J. CRANFORD

Forged Iron Press

Acknowledgments:

I've travelled to a fair amount of places. And met a lot of people. Experienced and seen a wide variety of things. I like to think, as I write, some of that comes through. That the world seems real. That even the smallest character feels alive.

So I want to thank all those along the road who've been a part of my life, whether for a few years or a few minutes. I hope, for those of you who read these stories, you find something of yourselves in them.

CHAPTER ONE

Master Sergeant Jason Bradley sat on a large flat rock. The mountains of Afghanistan stood tall above him. Scrublike brush dotted the hillsides, leaving splattered spots of brownish green to blot the hard browns of rocky cliffs and tan channels of stone. There was an arid feel to the air, like a desert, except that it was far colder here, even with the sun blazing overhead.

The foothills had been small at first. Like little rows stretched across the land. From the air they would have looked like a large hand lying on the ground, fingertips stretched far apart, as if the hand was trying to palm the earth. Then the fingers had swollen, the knuckles grown into rounded humps, tiny hillsides deepening into sharp ravines. Those ravines had gotten more treacherous, more vertical, until the hills had become true mountains, and then those had grown taller and taller, until they were deep in the Hindu Kush.

Killer of the Hindus, Jason thought. *And I wonder how many others....*

He focused on the small monastery below, the one McNulty had found the night before. Jason was dressed and kitted out in the Ranger camouflage, his rifle kicked up next to him, jacket tightly wrapped around him. The wind, when it gusted, held a sharp, bitter chill. One that cut through the jacket and the layered cloths Jason wore underneath.

He didn't like any of this. It was outside the norm of their usual assignments. Recons, target acquisitions, rescues, assassinations, his team had done them all. But reconning a town that seemed empty, a monastery that looked to have last seen use thousands of years ago, didn't make sense. Doubly so to do this assignment before coming in from the last one.

Their missions always began with a brief. Then the team would practice before hitting the field. Then the execution of the plan. Completing the mission and returning to home base.

The team almost never remained in a field after completion. This time, they had been able to get in a brief resupply as they were ordered to another assignment. And they had rushed out on that mission, without knowing the *whys* and *hows* and *whos* of it.

They just knew the where on this one. And Jason hadn't asked why, when given the assignment. He liked to know, because knowing always improved the success of a mission, but on the times he wasn't given the why, he rarely questioned the order. Answers to those questions were usually far above his pay grade. In those times, with those orders, he fell back to execution. That was his job, and he did that well. Had always done that well.

This time, though, Jason wished he had asked. Some people had showed up in a jeep this morning. Three of them, shortly after Jason's team had gotten there. Jason wasn't sure what they were doing. And the radios had stopped working the night before. Maybe this deep in the Kush, they would. So even if Jason reached out, no one would be listening.

He had a bad feeling about it.

His team was on edge, as well. Sue Franklin lay on the slope above them, rifle trained on the small town below. Her blond hair in a crew cut. Patrick lay next to her, spotting. Lilly Thompson was walking the perimeter with Gus McNulty, their newest member.

Joe Girogilia stood next to Bradley. His second-in-command for a long time. He was a big man, broad in the shoulder, thick in the chest. Normally the man had a five o'clock shadow a few minutes after a shave, but was sporting a brushlike beard now. Joe's machine gun, a compact MK-46, sat on a rock next to him.

"Still not sure?" his second-in-command asked. Joe's accent, Italian, always reminded Jason of New York. With its tall skyscrapers and crazy crowds and the smell of pizza at every corner.

Jason grunted. He and Joe had been together long enough that he knew Joe would take it as an assent. Still, Jason kept watch on the monastery below.

"Not a typical recon," Joe said. Joe, being Italian, was a natural-born talker. But in these moments, both of them knew what was ahead. The large problem in the mission. And so, when the two of them talked, it was something like this. Small sentences. Shorter words.

"No," Jason agreed. Normally they had clearly defined objectives. Someone to rescue. Someone to kill. Something to look at and report on. His eyes were still down the hill. "It is not."

The monastery lay below them, but above the floor of the foothills. Out of the way of where a river might have run, thousands of years ago. It had been cut into the side of the mountain, a square mud-brick thing. It stood multiple levels high, taller than the homes around it, formed from the same brick. Though they hadn't seen anyone, an old jeep was parked between two homes. A four-door vehicle, dusty and white.

The small town, or village, or whatever it was, seemed unobtrusive. Maybe like other towns Jason had seen, not towns in the Kush, but towns he had seen in Nevada. The old Indian homes carved into the red cliff-sides back there.

At the same time, this place seemed far older than those towns. It had been there a long time, the hard corners of the rock worn down by weather. Water erosion in places where there hadn't been water in a long time. The whole place seemed older than it should be. And old places in the Hindu Kush tingled something in Jason's brain. Old places were dangerous here.

"No insurgents," Joe added.

Jason sighed. "I don't know exactly what we're here for, either."

As far as Jason knew, no army regiment was headed this way. There was no reason for his team to be here, scouting this place. But he had a feeling there was a lot riding on this. His subconscious screamed *danger*, and whenever he felt that, the mission *did* get dangerous. Very often people died.

Jason wanted to keep his people from that, as much as he could.

"Call 'em?" Joe said.

Jason shook his head. "Don't think the radios'll work until we're out."

Radio comms had been out awhile. Then the team had gotten lost after the compasses went a little screwy. Jason wondered what else might go wrong. This felt like one of the stories he had read about the Bermuda Triangle. Communication out. Navigation screwy. He was flying blind and didn't know if he was going to land this thing or crash.

At least they had found the objective. What Home Base needed active reconnaissance on. So Jason and Joe sat on the hillside. Looking at the little village, carved out of the rock under the monastery. An old white jeep, topless, by the side of the building. Three people, a large man, a small man, and a thin man, had all at one point left the monastery to go to the jeep.

It was midday.

Jason wondered why he thought it was a monastery. His subconscious had identified it with the name. Maybe because it reminded him of one he had seen in Turkey. Stone. Carved. Thick. Multiple levels, with thick square windows high on each level. The building in Turkey had a dark roof, though. This one was the same color stone, and more square, then arched.

"Doesn't seem right," Joe said.

"No." Jason repeated himself. Which he never minded, if he was working through a thought. "It does not."

"Could be worse," Joe said, nodding to the northeast. "Could be up there."

Up there was the real Hindu Kush. The tall snow-peaked mountains, jagged tops pointing miles high in the air. Dark veins of stone, showing through the white snow here and there. Where Jason's team was now was on the edge, where the hills had become the mountains.

Joe was right; if this place had been up there, they couldn't have made it. Weren't kitted out for it. The bitter cold, the lack of oxygen, all that would have done them in.

Which only increased Jason's worry about this now. To send them here, low on supplies, spoke of critical timing. With what Jason knew about the world, that could be a very bad thing.

Joe grunted this time, patted Jason's shoulder. He was done saying his piece, and Jason was still working through his. Both he and Jason had been around the block a few times. They would get this done, too.

Down the hill from where Jason sat, Thompson and McNulty appeared. Doing their job well. Quiet steps. Smooth movements. Rifles held carefully at the ready. Careful turns of the head, searching the land around them.

McNulty was new. Relatively speaking. He had transferred to their division when they headed out for their turn in the rotation. But they had done enough missions now that he had blended in.

The Ranger was quiet, but intense. Dedicated. Worked with a ruthless efficiency Jason had seen in others. A man who got things done, as soon as they needed doing. Because he lived with a fear that not getting them done would get someone killed. And he was one of the best recon men Jason had been around.

Thompson came up. Her hair was a bit longer than normal, and she had it tied up in a ponytail under her helmet. It was the only thing out of standard with her. She was tall, thin, and athletic. Her shirt tucked neatly into her pants. Her jacket the perfect length. Her rifle at the proper angle, ready in her hands, pointed downhill. Everything just so.

"Nothing, Jason," she said.

Jason nodded. "Take a break."

"Yeah," Lilly snorted. She hadn't been happy at the extended mission. Christmas was coming around, and she was looking forward to getting back to Williamsburg, Virginia. This time of year, she was saying last night, they lit up the town with candles, drank sodas from metals cups. Jason didn't understand the attraction.

She clapped McNulty once on the back and headed back to camp, just a bit uphill. "Maybe I'll catch a movie or something."

Those two had gotten closer since Gus came on. Which Jason found interesting, because Lilly was five-dot-oh, and McNulty was never squared away. His shirt was usually untucked, his jacket open, sometimes even buttoned incorrectly. But he and Lilly were like brother and sister, almost. Closer for their differences.

McNulty still stood by Jason, not moving. The Ranger faced the monastery, below and across the ravine from them. Somewhere over a mile away.

It had been McNulty who found the place, the night before. After a few days of the team searching the hills for it. He had found it in the dead of night, with no moon or moonlight to see by, just the black sky above them holding thousands of pinpricks of stars.

If Jason only talked a little, McNulty might have been a mute. Which wasn't a knock on him. He was good, took the lead in every breach, did things with a silent, manic focus.

"Gus," Jason said quietly.

A few moments later. "Gus."

McNulty stared down at the village as if something there had spooked him. As if he was haunted. Possibly afraid. His rifle was slung around his back. McNulty had taken off his helmet and held it loosely in the crook of an arm. Like he was facing something ahead down there.

"Grimm," Jason finally said. Going to his nickname.

The soldier's head snapped up. Turned to face Bradley. Jason was always surprised at his eyes, an emerald green that at times turned a dark hazel, at times a brilliant sapphire. The change seemed to be mood-dependent. McNulty's hair was a mop of black wavy curls that seemed to grow back quickly after every haircut. His stare was fierce, but quiet. As if ready to challenge whatever Jason was about to ask.

So Jason didn't ask anything. He just nodded at the town. "Tell me, man."

Grimm looked back toward the monastery, then back. His expression became even more guarded. "Tell you what?"

"You found it," Jason said.

"Any of us could have," Grimm said.

"No." Jason shook his head. He traced the air with his finger, pointing out what he was saying. "You see the overhang. How it's tucked into that cliff. Three sides of the mountain around it. No way to see it from above. Even now, midday, it's covered in shadows. This place is as hidden as anything we've seen."

Grimm shrugged. "Luck, then."

Bradley didn't think it was luck. He had been facing Grimm the night before. The whole squad had been huddled in a circle. Talking through their search pattern. Wondering what they had missed.

Then Grimm's eyes had opened wide. Jason had recognized the expression as fear. He had looked west, straight to the monastery, miles away. And reluctantly had led them there. The soldier had wandered left and right a bit, like Grimm was still searching for the place, but Jason knew from the moment he had seen his face that he knew where it was. Jason knew he was hiding something then. And he was more convinced of it now.

"Grimm," Jason said, "I've seen this before."

"What?" he asked.

"People like you," Jason said.

Grimm pursed his lips, maybe to hide a snort. Or a chuckle.

Jason got the feeling Grimm thought there wasn't anyone else like him. So he tried to explain it in a way the man might get. "Look, man, I know the look of a person being chased by a demon. I've been in too many of these battles to not have seen it. Those people throw themselves into a fight. They're first in. Last out. Taking chances. Taking risks. As if daring someone to shoot them."

Jason paused a moment, catching Grimm's eyes. More of a hazel now. "As if daring someone to kill them."

Grimm's gaze flickered back and forth. Away from Jason's eyes, then back. His irises turning a dark hazel. "Are you saying I'm going to get someone killed?"

"That's not what I'm saying," Jason said.

"If you don't like how I operate," Grimm said, hot, "then pass me on. Like the last guy."

Interesting. Jason leaned forward, lowering his voice, but making sure he cut each word with the sharp edge of command. "You don't get the team killed. *I* get the team killed."

Grimm's eyes froze. He blinked, once, twice, maybe fighting something inside him. He set his jaw. "Sorry, Jay." The words came out rusty.

"It's fine, man," Jason told him. "We're all on edge. We all feel it. Something's different here. Something's different with this mission. So I need to figure it out, right? It's why I'm asking."

A few missions ago Patrick had gone down. Clearing a room. A shotgun had boomed as soon as Patrick entered, and the blast had taken him in the side. Even though Patrick had been wearing armor, he still had pebblelike scars along his skin today.

Grimm had hurdled Patrick almost immediately. Firing his rifle in short bursts. He stood over Patrick long enough that Jason could pull him back.

Jason had checked that room later. Each of Grimm's bursts had found a target. Four men, dead, hidden around the room. In places it would have been hard to see, behind furniture, doors. The man seemed to have a supernatural gift. Something not many others had.

"So, what, then, I'm not doing a good job?" Grimm asked.

It was Jason's turn to hold back a chuckle. Grimm was as good as anyone Jason had been around. He was naturally a fighter. He seemed to be born for it.

"That's not what I'm saying," Jason said. "I'm saying someone who lives on the edge of the fight, something happens to them. They work the edge so long they *feel* the battle around them. They *sense* what's coming. Maybe develop a premonition or two."

For a long moment, neither said anything. "I don't know what you're asking," Grimm finally said.

"I'm asking you to take a guess," Jason said. "I've been doing this a lot longer than you. I've ridden that same edge. I get feelings, too. And my gut is telling me that place is dangerous. That if we go down there, we're not coming back out."

"Then we don't go down," Grimm said. Maybe a little relieved.

Jason shook his head. "Right now I don't know what we're doing, other than a little recon. But I have to think of everything, man. Everything." Jason leaned forward, closer to Grimm, just a little, and lowered his voice. "And if you can help me keep our team alive, man, I want to hear what you think."

Grimm's eyes got wet. Which surprised Jason a little. But something inside the man was eating him alive, enough to make him emotional.

"What if it's not just a feeling?" Grimm said.

"Then tell me," Jason said.

There was a long moment when Jason thought Grimm would. Then he shook his head. "It'll sound crazy."

"I've seen crazy," Jason said.

And Jason had. He had stood in the middle of a fight, firing his M-4, with bullets and tracers raining down on his position, but leaving him untouched. He had seen Joe hold an alley on his own, against what seemed like a small army, until they had fled.

Grimm was different, though, and Jason wanted to know why. "So just tell me."

Another long pause from the Ranger. Jason could sense him hanging on the edge. As if wanting to tell someone his secret. Like it was eating Grimm alive, and he knew that all he had to do was talk about it, and he could survive whatever it was.

But Grimm still kept quiet. A minute passed. Another.

"All I'll say," Grimm finally said, "is something dark is down there. I'm pretty sure I've seen bad things. This thing, it's different. Bigger. Worse."

"But you don't know what it is?" Jason pressed.

Grimm shook his head. "No."

"But you know it's there?" Jason asked.

Grimm nodded once. "I do."

Jason could tell something was off about the place. Grimm telling him it was dangerous, it just made him feel worse about bringing his team down there. The best he could do was just keep them up here, watching. Jason shook his head. "I guess that's going to have to be enough."

A whistle split the air. Something brief and chittery. Hopefully something that sounded like a snowfinch, one of the birds of the Afghan.

Jason looked up the hill, where Patrick and Suzy were. Patrick held up two fingers, then pointed the fingers to the monastery. Jason looked down, seeing figures walk out of the monastery. So he pulled his rifle up and peered through its scope.

Two men stood outside. Both of them had dark hair and the swarthy tanned look of someone who had spent a lot of time in the sun. One of them, a bigger man outfitted in a flak jacket and strapped with weapons, went to the jeep and pulled out a bag. The other man, taller with sharp eyebrows and a hawklike expression, adjusted a dark red wool hat on his head.

The hat was soft, round, and a little floppy. Jason thought it was called a pakol cap. The tall man adjusted it, tucked some hair underneath one edge of the hat, then stood in front of the door. The hand shading his eyes. Staring west. Toward where Jason and his group hid.

Surely he can't see this far, Jason thought.

Pakol continued to stare the Ranger's way. Thick brown hair pushed out from under the edge of his hat; a thicker mustache covered his upper lip. The man looked to be in his forties, with deep lines at the corner of both eyes, the crow's-feet of someone who had spent a lot of time squinting.

Grimm went to one knee, also looking intently through his scope.

Jason tried one more time with the Ranger.

"You see them?" he asked Grimm.

Grimm nodded.

"What do they feel like to you?"

Grimm shook his head, as if he didn't know. "Nothing. Not dangerous."

"Nothing?" Jason asked.

Grimm repeated his headshake. He placed his rifle down, butt against the stony ground. His eyes, when he turned back to Jason, were that sapphire color again. Intense. Bright. As if he had seen something that interested him. "Not the bad feeling," Grimm finally said.

"But you did sense something else?" Jason asked.

Grimm waited a long moment. He let out a big breath. "Sometimes I feel colors."

"Colors?"

Grimm half rolled his eyes and gave a little shrug. "I know it sounds crazy. But it's like I know something is bad if I see red. Or purple. Or black." He shrugged, as if he couldn't explain it. Or didn't want to explain it further.

Grimm had said he felt colors, but then said he could *see* them. *Slip of the tongue, or something else?*

"Tell me," Jason said.

"That man," Grimm said. "The thin one? He was … he was green, I think."

"Green?" Jason asked.

"I know," Grimm answered, looking away, "sounds ridiculous."

Jason wished he had time to talk about it. He had heard rumors, from other teams, other missions. About things that went bump in the night. About other people that fought them. He had never given it much thought, but he had never outright dismissed the rumors, either. Jason listened to everything, took it all in, no matter how crazy or ridiculous. Then he would weigh the data, pull what he could from it, and make the decisions needed to keep his team alive.

This whole thing has been ridiculous, Jason thought. *From getting the mission. Almost on the fly. Like it was unimportant. Yet this feels like it's about to go south, and I can't see how or why.*

"So, is green good, then?" Jason asked Grimm.

Grimm, still looking away, nodded. "As far as I can tell, green usually means something at least … not bad."

Jason got on himself. *For God's sake, man. It's just two people. A quick recon of a few empty houses. If you have to go down there, you'll go down there. Get the job done.*

He didn't want to, though. He could feel that, for sure. His instincts screamed it at him.

Jason looked through his scope again. The man with the pakol was talking to the larger man. They both gestured to the monastery. Pakol shook his head, and the bigger man argued a bit further, heading back to the jeep. Pakol grabbed him and pointed back to the monastery.

The big man stomped his way in, carrying the bag.

Pakol looked out to the hills one more time. His gaze traveled the sky, pausing maybe over Jason's team. Then pausing a bit farther north, before Pakol shook his head and headed back inside.

Jason took his rifle and looked north. There was a dark smudge on the horizon there. Right over the crest of the hills there. It was small, a blue-black dime against the background of the sky, but it was there. As Jason watched, the smudge swelled slightly. As if growing larger. Or closer.

Jason pulled his rifle down. To the naked eye the smudge was barely visible. The ridge of the hillside was a couple of miles away, at least. How had that man known it was there?

"Grimm," Jason said. His voice no longer thoughtful, but commanding.

The Ranger recognized it. "Sergeant."

"Take Thompson and check out that smudge up north." Jason wondered how much more he could tell him. So he stressed the final word, and made sure to look Grimm in the eye. *"Carefully."*

Grimm tilted his head a bit, then nodded. He looked north and west, toward the smudge, one hand over his eyes. Shading them from the sun, descending in the west. Grimm looked long and hard, then let out a breath before heading over to where Lilly was sitting cross-legged, at the back of their camp.

"FlowerPower," Grimm joked. "How's that movie?"

Lilly had lain back in the brush, flat and looking up at the sky. Maybe taking a moment of rest. "Fuck you, Grimm, I heard him."

"Then you know I'm waiting on you," Grimm said, grinning.

Of the whole team, Lilly was the only person the Ranger was a little relaxed around. Otherwise, he was business. Lethal in battle. But dangerous as well. Jason thought Grimm was a good man. But no one threw himself so hard at the enemy, so many times, unless he was trying to right a wrong. Unless he was screaming out to the world, *Kill me or absolve me*.

Those kinds of people could get others killed.

So Jason wondered how much he could trust what Grimm had told him. What the soldier was hiding from him. He wondered if the smudge had a color as well. And wondered if Grimm was here to help him or get his team killed.

CHAPTER TWO

Grimm and Thompson had been gone an hour before Jason heard the first gunshots. A steady pattern, break, and pattern. Controlled bursts from automatic rifles. The sounds worried Jason, but they also comforted him.

He had used the M-4 everywhere, and the sounds were not panicked. Whatever the two had found, they were handling it as well as they could. Even when staccato-fire, single sharp rounds answered the bursts. Then a few minutes before the next burst.

That they had found something, though, was worrisome.

Jason tried his comms unit. Still nothing but static. Jason checked with Joe, across the way from him, and Joe nodded. Girogilia had heard him over his portable radio. So Grimm and Thompson might be out of range.

The whistle of the snowfinch again. Suzy and Patrick still watched the monastery. Jason looked back down. The man with the pakol had come back out, and stared north for a moment. Then glanced back at where Jason's team hid. A third man came out, a thinner guy, smaller than the other big man. The two of them talked for a bit, then went back inside.

Green, Grimm had said. Whatever the fuck that meant. Jason had seen some crazy things out here. In battle. Might as well add rainbow colors to it.

It was getting darker faster. The sun had descended quickly in the west, and night was coming just as fast. Even now the once-yellow orb had become a burning red disk, slipping over the horizon.

Joe came over. He nodded to the north. The way the hill they were on was curved, the smudge would crest the ridgeline and skirt the edge of a sharp fall until whatever it was came on Jason and his team. They were smack-dab in the middle of the only slope that could be navigated, down to the town.

Jason didn't like that. And he didn't like that the town would be the only place they could hole up. But beggars couldn't be choosers.

Jason motioned to the town with his head. Joe nodded and took off, carrying the machine gun like it weighed nothing. The two of them understood Jason wanted them all back at the town. It was the only defensible spot around.

But they both knew what that would mean.

"Q, Ice," Jason said. He always felt nicknames gave his Rangers a power. Like they were all the same person, working on the same wavelength, working the same limbs. A tight family. A deeper connection than the formal use of last names, or the anonymous alphanumeric and number assignment. "Pack up."

"Town?" Patrick asked, holding his shotgun across his legs. A short Benelli. He had been etching something into the metal, just above the trigger.

Jason nodded.

"No place for me," Suzy-Q said, still lying prone in front of her rifle.

"There isn't," Jason agreed.

Suzy cursed softly. Jason smiled. She was as good a sniper as he had known, and she loved her MK-11. Lying on the ground, centering the target in the scope. Suzy had that connection, the feel, of how a round traveled through the air, how gravity and wind affected its passage. A natural.

"Maybe the top of the monastery," he suggested. "When we get there."

Her eyes lit up. Suzy-Q was good. Every sniper was different, in Jason's experience. But they all—when it came down to pulling the trigger—had that ability to center themselves. To eliminate all the distractions around them. To take the science of the wind and elevation and distance and throw that into the back of their minds, to add intuition and a certain *feel*, and hit their target.

And every sniper loved that moment.

The three of them packed up the supplies, ammo, and weapons. They shouldered the extra packs of their teammates. The controlled bursts of McNulty and Thompson always in the background. Single shots answered, and then more concentrated fire. Occasionally there was a boom and a rumble. And then, as Jason and the pair with him headed down to the town, he heard Gorilla's machine gun thumping its way through whatever the three of them faced.

Joe had made it there.

And things were getting worse.

The three Rangers made their way down to the town. They traversed the ground quickly. Joe had been right—things would have been more difficult had they been higher in the Hindu Kush. They would have had to relay and climb and take their time to pull their extra gear up. But here, at least, they followed what Jason thought was an old riverbed, from maybe a glacier melting hundreds of thousands of years ago, until they crossed the ravine and stood in front of the town.

Up close the buildings in the town seemed much older than when Jason had eyed them through his rifle's scope. As if being there in person brought some age into play. Up on the hill the town had seemed staged like a movie, with the slight weathering of buildings long abandoned. But now that he was next to them, Jason could clearly see the pockmarked rock, from rains over thousands of years. The etching of water into the stone steps of the buildings, where water had once run alongside, year after year. Even indentations in the path leading up to the monastery, where people had trod, over and over, year after year, until a tiny channel of footprints had been carved into the walkway.

This place has a history, Jason thought.

And it was like nothing else he had seen in Afghanistan. Or the Kush. There were more people living in caves, man-made or otherwise, in the hills than a town like this.

Pakol had come out, watching the team as they approached. Occasionally the man would glance north, at the firefight. Once, the big man came out, again arguing, and then went back inside.

The third man stepped out as well, the thinner man with the ponytail.

He remained as the team got closer, a grim smile pasted on his face, eyes constantly flicking to the cliff, as if Ponytail couldn't stop looking. As if something pulled him that way.

Jason found himself wishing Grimm was here. He wanted to know what colors each of the men were, if all of them were green. Grimm said he felt a darkness here. It was something Jason felt, too. He wondered if it was the building, or something else. Something darker, even sinister.

The three of them slowed down as they approached the monastery, until they stopped, twenty or thirty feet away. The building, only four stone levels, seemed much taller now that they stood below. The thin man headed back inside. The big man stood in the shadow of the doorway, holding an AK-47 in both hands, with the barrel pointed down.

Pakol waited until Jason stopped, then nodded.

"English?" Jason asked.

Pakol made a so-so motion with his hand. "A little," he said. "My friends, no."

Jason pointed up north. "What do you know about that?"

Pakol pursed his lips. His eyes narrowed, as if in thought. "I know it is bad."

Jason thought this man might be the person with the package he needed to retrieve. He wanted to break radio silence and ask more questions, any question. Irrationally he wanted to ask Pakol about it, or maybe just take it and run. By force, if he had to. A deep fear had come over him, that today was going to be his last day on earth.

But he had had those feelings before. So he pushed them down now. Whether or not Jason lived, he was going to make sure his team survived. And a running firefight down the side of the mountain was not going to accomplish that.

"It's coming this way," Jason said.

"Yes," Pakol agreed.

"Going to be rough," Jason said.

"Yes," Pakol said again.

"Mind if we come in?" Jason said. "Maybe we can weather it together?"

Pakol looked puzzled. Jason realized it was at the word *weather*. So he swung his rifle to point to the north, and mimed pulling the trigger, trying to explain. "Team up."

"Oh," Pakol said, then smiled. He was missing one of his front teeth, but the smile was large and friendly. "I must ask, why?"

"Why?" It was Jason's turn to be puzzled.

"Why here?" Pakol said. "You."

Jason stared at him for a long moment.

"You have mission?" Pakol asked.

Jason realized then. Swore. "You knew about this."

Pakol's smile lessened, became sad. "Yes."

The bad feeling along Jason's spine deepened, became a cold pressure along his back.

"How?" Jason asked.

"It is how it passes," Pakol said. "When the time nears."

"How *what* passes?" Jason said. "Do you need something carried?" Was this why Jason was here? The purpose of his vague recon orders? He nodded to his team. "Give it to us. We'll take it and run."

Pakol tilted his head, and Jason mistook that for puzzlement, so he tried to explain by waggling his fingers, like he was running. "We will run. Carry. For you."

Pakol laughed then, but it was a short, bitter laugh. "I cannot."

"We can." Jason took a step closer, and the big man raised his AK-47. Jason sensed Patrick and Suzy about to do the same, and waved them both down.

"You misunderstand," Pakol said. "It is not for me to choose."

"Jason," Patrick interrupted.

The shooting had gotten much closer. Still controlled bursts, rotating. His team taking turns. With the occasional long punctuation of the machine gun.

Patrick had pointed to the cliff, high to the north. The ridge that ran north to south, before being weathered into the slope Jason had just walked down. Three figures stood there, one of them casting a long rope down the side of the mountain. One figure kneeling, firing bursts out of his rifle. It might have been Grimm.

They were going to take a shortcut.

Jason swore. They weren't going to run from anything. If Joe was doing that, there wasn't any time left.

The first figure started rappelling down, with an economy of motion and precision that Jason knew was Lilly. Which meant Joe and Grimm were still up top.

The hill to the west had obscured the sun, but it must have burned a fiery red, because the entire horizon blazed with it. At least until the sky reached the north, where the darkness had swollen larger and larger, blotting out everything.

The machine gun again. There was some motion between the two men up top. Like they were arguing. One of them, it must have been Grimm, slapped a new magazine into his rifle and turned back to fire. And as Jason watched, things started jumping off the cliff to the left and right of the men. Bodies, human beings maybe, though they were small and tumbled almost like figures from a Claymation movie.

The argument halted between the men. Joe stopped firing his machine gun, slung the thing over his back, and began his descent next. With bodies falling to his left and right, and Grimm up top, still firing at something. And still the darkness swelling behind the men, overflowing them, pouring down the cliff.

What the hell? Jason wondered. And maybe he had said it aloud, because Patrick turned to look back at him.

"The *scourge*," Pakol whispered. His face was very pale, though his jaw was set.

"You know this?" Jason asked.

Pakol nodded. "You are welcome in, my friends," he said as tiny thumps of bodies smacked against rock, as the tat-tat-tatting of an assault rifle echoed down the chasm. "Together, may we find some peace."

Peace. Jason shook his head. As in *resting in peace.* Pakol had put on a brave face, but he did not expect to live long.

"Holy …," Patrick said.

Grimm had latched himself to the rope while he was firing his last magazine. With a shout, the soldier flung himself off the back of the cliff, tumbling down the rope a ways before somehow jerking to a halt. His assault rifle dropped out of his hand. Jason tracked it and watched it bounce off the rock side.

Bodies followed. They poured over the edge, as if someone had a gigantic cup of the creatures, and the cup had tipped over, flooding the cliff. A few bounced off Grimm. One grabbed hold, there was motion between them, and then the body fell off.

Grimm worked his way down quickly. Jason watched him slide until he thought it was too fast, then maybe even reckless, and then jerking to a stop. Bouncing on the rope.

Joe's machine gun kicked up again, bullets firing up past Grimm, tiny zips of bullets tearing through the crowd above. Some part of Jason's mind tracked the sounds, listened to the echoes, and estimated how far away they were.

Maybe twenty, maybe thirty minutes.

Grimm kept sliding, until Jason lost him from sight.

He looked around. Patrick stood as if lost, his face slack. Staring at what was happening in perhaps wonder. Perhaps fear.

Suzy wasn't much different. Her eyes narrowed. As if she was measuring distances, for shots.

"Patrick," Jason said. Then, "Johnson."

The man stared, his fingers loosely wrapped around his shotgun. A tiny cross etched into the metal of the barrel above Patrick's thumb.

"Patty Ice," Jason said loudly.

Patrick shook himself, then looked over at Jason. It was a silly nickname that Suzy had given him, but the man had always been calm, under pressure. Like ice. Not now, though. Not today.

He nodded. "Jason."

"Get the claymores out," Jason said. Pointing to corners of buildings, where tiny alleys headed to the monastery, from the west. "Get the entrances to those. Every corner you can. Make us a wall."

"Got it." Patrick grabbed his pack, and Joe's and Grimm's and Thompson's. Pulling out all the explosives they carried. In the back of his mind Jason knew they had six claymores. Which, with luck, would be enough.

Whatever those things were, they weren't paying attention to things like bullets. It looked like they charged, and charged, and then charged some more. With any hope, they would funnel through the alleys, hit the claymores, and collapse the buildings.

It would be an early warning system, of sorts. And a delaying tactic. Each alley they collapsed, those *scourges* would have to find another way. Until all those bodies had left to run through was the single street, heading up to the monastery. The street Jason was standing on now. A more defensible position.

Jason caught Suzy's eye. She had already turned from watching the cliff.

"Up top?" she said, motioning her head to the monastery.

Jason nodded. "We got maybe twenty minutes. Escort our team in, would you?"

"You got it, chief," Suzy said, and headed into the monastery. Past the man with the AK-47, who, although he also looked up at the cliff, still scowled. As if friendly to none. Pakol turned to watch Suzy go, waving off his big friend.

"You called these things a *scourge*?" Jason asked.

Pakol looked back. His face still pale, his eyes steady. "Yes."

"You've seen this before?"

Pakol shook his head. "These things are … only a tale."

No help there, Jason thought. *No information to be had*. He looked at the jeep. "What do you have?"

"Myself," Pakol said, then nodded at the big man. "Sameer. And Zahir. Us three."

Sameer slung his rifle on his back. He made a motion with both hands, two fists together, then opening both. "Boom."

More explosives. Jason looked at Sameer. "Where?"

"The jeep," Pakol answered for the big man.

Jason ran over to it. In the back was another bag, a big canvas duffel bag. Inside were blocks of C-4, detonators, cable. Which had him grinning. They might have a chance with this.

He tugged the bag out and over the lip of the jeep's side panel. It was heavy. Quickly he looked around and did the math. Distance from the monastery. Number of blocks. Placement. The big man, Sameer, came down next to Jason, motioning to help, and Jason directed him where he wanted the blocks.

If they couldn't get them all, he thought, at least they would go out with a bang.

CHAPTER THREE

The monastery was basically four larger rooms, one on top of another. Tiny square windows circled the top of each room, maybe so people could see, or maybe it was just for air. The rooms were unlit, full of shadows and only getting darker, cut through by beams of fading light from a dying sun on the western wall.

Jason ran his hand over the stone. It felt smooth, like a pebble in a riverbed, worn by thousands of years of water flowing over it. There were none of the pockmarks he saw on the outside, or in the town.

And it was quiet inside. Much quieter than outside. Maybe it was the thick walls, but there were still the windows. The muffled bursts of assault rifles from his team, rushing ahead of the scourge, were only punctuated by large, sonic booms of Suzy overhead.

"Where can we help?" Pakol asked.

Jason pointed to the second floor. He didn't want anyone not on his team on the first floor. That was going to be where the rubber met the road, and he wanted people who were used to fighting together to take the first wave. "Have Sameer guarding the stairs."

Pakol nodded.

"Does Zahir have a gun?" Jason asked.

"A pistol," Pakol said.

That wasn't going to be enough, Jason thought. Wondering, briefly, at why these three men were together. And here. Who they were. And if it would even matter.

"How do we kill these *scourges*?" Jason asked.

Pakol frowned. "They are already dead."

Jason wanted to laugh, but didn't. He had watched them tumbling themselves over the cliff. He pointed to his own temple with his first two fingers, bringing his thumb down. "Shot to the head?" *Like a zombie movie?*

Pakol shrugged. "There is a rakshasa with them," he said. "It is he who you must shoot."

Jason didn't know what a rakshasa was. Or a scourge. Maybe, if they all came out of this alive, he could ask then. "Take the stairs on the third floor."

Pakol tilted his head, as if asking a question. Jason took a breath and explained, slowly, motioning with his hands, "Go up two stairs. Wait for us there."

"I understand," Pakol said, and smiled. It was a bright smile, for so dark a place. The man's eyes were clear of sadness, and focused. "Find peace, brother."

Jason snorted. "Peace is for the dead." Which, of course, they all could be, soon enough.

Pakol went up the stairs, pulling Sameer with him. Jason had not seen Zahir since the first time, when he had come out the door. Patrick passed Pakol on the stairs, shifting a little to the side to allow him by.

He held his shotgun in one hand, and his rifle on his back. Patrick nodded a question at the door. "There?"

"You got it," Jason said. He wanted the Benelli there, keeping the entryway clear until the rest of their team got back in. "When Joe gets here, you can hop it up top."

The doorway was blocked off with the jeep, the only thing in the town they could find. It was parked sideways across the door, leaving a tall gap at the top and a smaller gap at the bottom. They had cut the tires so that the vehicle lay as low to the ground as it could. Jason wished they had had the time to tilt it over sideways. But at least it was something.

They would hold the door first. Then the team would move up, floor by floor. There were stone stairs at the back of the building. The steps folded back on top of themselves at each level.

Whatever this scourge was, there were a lot of them. Jason hoped that they could outlast it. This battle would be one of attrition. The first thing they would likely run out of was bullets. Hand-to-hand would follow soon after that. The fight was going to be brutal. Bloody.

They would have to hold out as long as they could. Simple as that.

"Here they come," Patrick said, taking his place to the side of the doorway.

A few loud shots from the top of the monastery cut through the air. The machine gun had stopped firing. There was just the sound of one assault rifle, and the bursts were erratic. But sounding closer. Right outside.

Jason stood ready, by the packs and the ammo. His rifle on his back. The detonator looped around his belt.

There was a big explosion outside. To the north. One of the alleyways, then. The monastery didn't shake, but the boom of the explosion carried through the air, and the echo of it called over and over as the sound traveled up the mountainside.

There was a scrambling sound of boots over metal. Thumping as someone jumped onto the hood of the jeep. And then Joe came through.

The Italian was covered in black blood. As if he had opened up his gun with those bodies right in front of him. The ichor had spattered back over his clothes, his face, his helmet.

He took a big breath, wiped his face, and sighed. He spotted Jason. "We got trouble."

"I know." Jason held out Gorilla's pack. "You good?"

Joe nodded and took his pack. The Ranger reloaded his gun, taking quick stock of the room. In the darkening sun, there wasn't much to see, but he did spot the stairs, assessing the situation and figuring out the plan. "Floor by floor?"

Jason nodded.

"Claymores were a good idea," Joe said.

"Buys us time," Jason said.

Joe laughed, and it was a bitter, choking thing. Short, and cut off quickly. "The guy with the cap?"

"Third floor," Jason said. "Big guy with an AK on the second."

Joe nodded. "I'll take the bottom of the steps."

It would be a good place to fire the machine gun from, when it all went to hell.

"Careful," Jason said. "He doesn't speak English."

"Shit, Jay." Joe held up his gun. "Everyone speaks this."

"There's something out there controlling these things," Jason said. "We have to find him and kill him."

Joe nodded again. As if that was a normal task, on a normal mission.

More scrambling over the jeep. A figure tumbled in, dragged off the hood by Patrick. Grimm. The soldier was covered in black ichor, like Joe, but his face had been scraped badly, and red blood mixed with the black. Grimm stumbled over behind Patrick, leaning over, his hands on his knees. Either hurt, or tired, or both.

A second claymore exploded. One last burst from Lilly's assault rifle, and then more boots over the jeep. Lilly fell in quickly, as if she had jumped and slid over the hood, like in the cop shows.

Patrick stood behind her, raising the Benelli and pulling the trigger a few times. There was a ripping, tearing sound, and a splat of liquid dotted the jeep.

"Hell, Grimm." Lilly grinned, patting the Ranger on the back. "You tired?"

Grimm swore, but grinned back at Lilly. He was bent over, hands on his knees, trying to catch his breath. It was a maniac move, jumping off the cliff the way he had done. But Grimm lived for the fight, always pressed his limits. Jason had always known that.

Another boom, in the background. Another claymore. More echoes of the explosion, rumbling up the cliffs. Then a moment of silence.

Then another round from Suzy's sniper rifle.

And another claymore exploding.

"Listen up, people," Jason said. "Going to be rough. We're going to hold here, then go two by two up the stairs."

"Going to be a bloodbath," Lilly said.

"It's fine," Jason said. "As long as it's their blood."

"I lost my rifle," Grimm said, leaning back against the wall. He had also lost his helmet in his fall. His face was a mess of dirt, grime, and blood, and all of that streaked up into his hair.

Patrick handed him the Benelli and a pack holding ammo. "Don't lose her."

Grimm nodded, flipping the weapon around in his hands, checking the load.

Patrick unslung his rifle and looked up, asking the question.

"You guys look for something controlling these things," Jason told Patrick. "Tell Suzy to take it out. Anything hanging around the back that looks different."

"Got it," Patrick said, and got ready to go.

Jason held him up with a hand on his shoulder. "There's a good chance it's going to be on you guys to get this thing," he told Patrick. "Keep Suzy clean."

Patrick nodded and took off, taking the stairs two at a time. Even as he did, there was another boom from the roof, and one of the last claymores went off, immediately after.

Jason waited until the echoes of the blast died down.

"Grimm, hold the door. Lilly, take one of the back corners," he told his team. "I'll take the other. Joe's at the bottom of the steps. Once Grimm can't keep the door clear, it's on us."

They all nodded. Lilly took her corner. There was the steady *click-clack* of Rangers loading their guns, checking weapons, that always happened before a fight.

"You good, Grimm?" Lilly's voice came from her corner.

"Good enough," the soldier replied. Leaning against the wall, running a hand through his hair. "You?"

"Just tell me when to start screaming *Game Over, Man!*" Lilly replied.

Grimm chuckled from his corner. "That's a good movie." Grimm leaned back against the corner of the wall by the door, maybe resting a moment, but still looking out the doorway to the west.

"Grimm, when you lose the door, pull back," Jason said. "We'll cover you. Then it's floor by floor. You guys know the drill."

"Got it," Grimm said. Lilly echoed him.

Jason was proud of his team. They faced something far out of the ordinary. Maybe supernatural. And they got ready for it like a well-oiled machine.

"You guys heard me tell Patrick. There's something out there controlling whatever these things are," Jason told them. "We get him, we get them."

"Know what it looks like?" Lilly asked.

"Nope," Jason said. "They don't give us easy. You guys keep an eye out, though. I'm hoping it just looks different than these things. Maybe we get a chance."

He looked at Grimm when he said that. Wondering if it was one of the odd colors the man could see. Or feel. Whatever it was he did.

Grimm seemed to understand, and he nodded carefully at Jason. His eyes were narrowed, as if he was in thought.

"Just a big game of whack-a-mole," Joe said, with a grin. "And they only have the one hole."

"Easy enough," Jason said, taking his corner. Getting on one knee. "Going to be frantic, people. Stay sharp. Controlled bursts. Careful with each other."

"Got it," they all said.

The last of the sun died out then. The little light they had in the room faded away, each of the tiny square openings in the west dimming out. Jason flicked his night vision on, and heard the rest of his team doing the same. The world appeared like a video game before him, sharp green outlines of shapes, red and yellow bodies, all wrapped up in a fuzzy, staticky darkness.

"Grimm?" Lilly asked the question. He had lost his helmet.

"I'm good," the Ranger answered.

Colors, Jason thought. Grimm would see what he needed to see in colors. Then Jason shivered, and wondered if Grimm could hold the door.

Actually the question wasn't if the Ranger could hold the door. It was just for how long.

A light thudding came from outside. Like someone driving cattle, hooves pounding the ground. The sound swelled larger and larger until Jason could almost feel the rumble in his feet.

But no screaming. No shouting. That was eerie.

Grimm stayed by the door. He still looked west. His voice steady as he kept up the chatter with Lilly. "How's the movie over there?"

"Fuck you," Lilly said, but there was a grin in her voice.

"Hard to believe you watched *Aliens*," Grimm said. "I always thought you were more of an *Ever After* girl."

"You know that's your favorite," Lilly said.

"Stay sharp, people," Jason said, but lightly. Just a reminder.

He watched Grimm. The Ranger was outlined in green now in Jason's night vision. He had braced himself against the wall, like Patrick had before. The shotgun held high against one shoulder, the barrel wedged between his hand and the edge of the doorway. His eyes wide-open, searching. Shaking his head now and then.

A keening had broken out outside. A wailing that almost sounded like wings fluttering. Like the whisper of wind, cutting through a chasm. Like a million locusts, descending through the air.

Joe took a large breath, next to Jason. He patted his MK, waiting. The last claymore went off outside. It was followed by a few more shots by Suzy, up top. A little chattering of Patrick's M-4.

And then Grimm.

"Here they come," the man said by the door, right when Jason heard thumps of bodies on the metal of the jeep.

The Benelli had seven shots. They went quickly. After the last shot Grimm swiveled to the corner by the door. Lilly covered him then while Grimm reloaded.

It all looked unreal, in the ghostlike green of the night-vision goggles. The bodies of the scourge were lit only faintly, just the edges of fingers and arms, in one particular case the sharp outline of an emaciated face, a jutting cheekbone. Whatever these things were, Jason didn't feel like they were human anymore.

They are already dead, Pakol had said. And Jason was beginning to believe him. They needed whatever the rakshasa was. In a movie, it would be some creature far in the back of the scourge, dressed differently in robes, maybe glowing some color and levitating in the air. Probably chanting.

Jason didn't think real life would work that way. If these scourges were being controlled, and the thing controlling them was out there, well, they would have to be really lucky. Or—Jason touched the detonator on his belt—or they would have to take as many as they could with them.

Grimm went back to the door. He weighed and measured each load for maximum effect, trying to catch as many of the monsters in one shot as possible. The booms of the Benelli echoed in the small room, but the wailing outside increased, as if more and more of the creatures surrounded the building.

The shotgun went empty again. Grimm ducked back in his corner.

Jason's turn. He lined up his rifle and plucked out heads as they appeared. Firing short bursts each time a body showed on the top of the jeep.

The jeep itself began to rock. Lilly fired a few times, catching some of the scourges that were pushing through, underneath the vehicle. More and more pressed into the opening.

Grimm swiveled back. He was inches from a few of the creatures, but stood sharp and pulled the trigger, pushing the gun's barrel out over the hood of the vehicle, blowing the scourge back, trying to keep the door free. At one point Grimm was leaning completely over the jeep, one foot on a tire rim, firing the shotgun with one hand, his KA-BAR knife in his other.

Say what you will about Grimm maybe having a death wish, Jason thought. Reloading his own rifle. The man could hold a door. He could fight.

Then Grimm was empty again. He pulled back. At the last second he tugged on his foot, like it was trapped. Jason saw ghostly green outlines of fingers on his boot.

Lilly snapped off a shot, and the fingers retreated.

Grimm nodded at her. Lilly fired more. Grimm reloaded. Jason picked up any slack. Joe waited for his turn.

Jason's team was good. They knew each other well, worked together like a well-oiled machine. Like they had been doing this exact fight all their lives. Rinse and repeat.

Grimm reloading again. Both Jason and Lilly covering him now. Alternating who had top and bottom of the jeep. Grimm was dripping in the black ichor, and wiped his eyes quickly with the back of an arm. It didn't do anything but smear his face. A hand pushed through, between the side of the jeep and the wall, and tried to reach back inside the door for Grimm.

Jason took it off with a shot. The elbow hung in the air, twitching. Pinned between the jeep and the wall. Jason had no idea how the body of the scourge had even fit where it was now stuck.

Each time one of the creatures appeared, bodies gaunt, dressed in rags, Jason fired a burst. Until Joe tapped him on the shoulder. Lightly.

Jason looked at where Joe pointed. The tiny square windows ringing the floors. The walls of the monastery were almost two feet thick, and the windows cut in the tops of those walls were each maybe the size of a small moving box. Maybe something a six- or seven-year-old kid could climb through.

The scourges pushed their bodies through each one, forcing themselves to fit in the tiny holes. Black blood leaked from all the windows as the creatures tried to push themselves through the small tunnels of stone. Skin tore. Limbs broke. Pieces of limbs tumbled to the floor. But still the monsters kept pressing through.

What the fuck? Jason thought. Then pointed it out. "Lilly."

She looked too, and immediately started firing into each window. Short bursts that quickly followed each other. There were just too many. Covering the windows and Grimm was going to be too much. Jason turned back just in time to watch Grimm spin back to his corner to reload.

"Get ready, Joe," he said while firing.

"Yep," the Italian said.

"Grimm," Jason shouted. The doorway was full of bodies, some moving, most of them not. Bodies torn open and lying there, on top of each other, wrapped in rotten, dirty clothes. The pieces slowly pushed inward, at the door, by the number of creatures trying to get in from behind the jeep.

Grimm finished reloading, glancing at Jason. The Ranger looked at the windows, summing up the situation.

"Pull back," Jason shouted.

Grimm stepped into the doorway a final time. Firing the Benelli as fast as he could. Jason and Lilly fell back quickly, to the stairs. Behind Joe, who knelt at the bottom step, machine gun propped on his knee.

Lilly ran up. Jason waited. Grimm swiveled one last time, pressing himself against the wall and working himself back to the stairs.

A moment later a flood of bodies pushed in over the jeep's hood, tumbling into the doorway.

Joe opened fire. Bursts of light illuminated Jason's night-vision goggles. The MK tore the scourges apart. Bullets thundered into the crowd at the door. Pieces of the creatures blew off and flew everywhere. As Joe fired, a fine black mist grew and hung around the doorway.

Still, the creatures came. The machine gun thundered. Grimm made it to the stairs, tapping Joe on the shoulder as he passed.

Joe quit firing, hauling his gun up quickly. The three Rangers retreated to the second floor, passing Sameer at the top. The big man still wore his scowl, as if that was the only way his face would go, but he nodded at the Rangers as they passed.

One floor down. Three to go. Jason felt along his belt, making sure the detonator was there.

Someone tapped his shoulder. Grimm. "I didn't see anything different out there," the Ranger told him.

Jason nodded, then pointed up. "Get up there with Q and Ice."

Grimm nodded, running up the stairs. Maybe they would get lucky, and find whatever this rakshasa thing was, though Jason was beginning to doubt it. He choked on a laugh, bitter in his throat, wondering how he had gotten into a place where he was trying to find some mythical creature a guy in a pakol cap had told him about, so he could keep his team alive.

Sameer opened fire. The AK had a different sound, thumpier, than the Ranger's assault rifles. Joe reloaded, to the side, but Lilly joined Sameer and fired into the crowd below. Jason pointed his rifle and fired as well.

The scourges had flooded into the first floor, filling it from top to bottom, their bodies pressed so tightly together they looked like a black wave of water, flowing to the stairs. Each of the creatures climbed upon another, so much so it appeared as if the ones at the top were swimming a dark surge. They pushed inward, swelling to the stairs, pressing up each step, only the briefest flash of fingers or a face in Jason's night vision.

Otherwise, it was all dark. Blackness. Something that would swallow his team whole.

The three of them kept firing. Jason found himself screaming, until his magazine emptied. Joe tapped him on the shoulder, pulling him back and taking his place in a quick movement, pointing the MK down into the crowd and letting go.

"Last mag," Joe shouted.

The thundering of the machine gun echoed loud along the walls. The sound reverberated to the Rangers, and the sheer number of bullets tearing into the creatures pushed them back, for a brief moment.

They weren't going to hold this floor. Not for five minutes. Not even for a minute. Just until Joe ran out of bullets.

"Third floor," Jason shouted, pulling Sameer and pushing the big man to the next set of stairs. Pushing Lilly along, too. Then he pulled a frag grenade out.

Joe fired until his gun was empty. The broken and bleeding bodies began working their way up the stairs again. The Italian swore and threw his gun at the topmost creature, jumping back.

"Fire in the hole!" Jason tossed the frag below. He and Joe raced around the opening of the floor, around to where the steps folded back on themselves, heading to the third floor.

A muffled thump shook the floor briefly. Pieces of bodies flew up into the second floor, followed by a wet spat of black liquid. As if hundreds of bodies had packed themselves tightly around the frag, so tight the explosion had been contained, just burping up the scourges that had been closest to the grenade.

They made it to the third floor. Pakol stood there, with three cylindrical tanks on his back. And a flamethrower in his hands, the flame a bright green glow in Jason's night vision. The men must have had it in the pack they had pulled from the jeep earlier.

There's your green, Grimm, Jason thought, wildly. Laughing out loud. *Whatever the fuck it means.*

Pakol nodded at Jason, his forehead beaded in sweat. His eyes narrowed, the man's gap-tooth smile replaced by a tight grimace.

Lilly slung her shotgun off her back and tossed it to Joe, who took a position behind Pakol, against the wall, so he could fire diagonally down the stairs. Lilly a step back from Joe.

"This is crazy," Lilly said.

Joe lay back against the wall, breathing heavy, and nodded.

"It is what it is," Jason said. "We just have to kill it."

"It is evil," Pakol said. "All we can do is stand against it."

Jason felt the detonator on his belt and wondered, in the press of bodies outside, if even all that C-4 would work. *How many of them are there?*

The keening of the scourge got louder, echoing in from outside, bouncing along the roads. It only got louder, and like a car alarm, the sound pierced Jason's ears. He winced, looking around.

They would have to get to the top. Draw as many as they could into the building now. Run to the roof. Blow the C-4. Hope that the explosion got this rakshasa thing, somehow. Hope Jason had calculated correctly, and the monastery didn't collapse with it. Hope his team could survive it all and make it out.

Seemed like a tall order. And with that, something in Jason snapped.

Not that he was panicked, he never panicked, but a calmness settled over him.

The realization of death is a powerful thing, he thought. *Whatever these creatures want, whatever they are here for, all we can do is stand against them for as long as we can.*

The scourge appeared below, at the foot of the stairs. The first few creatures climbed up the stairs. Joe blew them back with the shotgun. More creatures piled up, and Joe kept shooting. Until the entire second floor was packed with the monsters.

Pakol screamed and let loose with the flamethrower. Large bursts of flame rolled down the stairs, picking up on the old rags the bodies wore, their dry skin, muscle, old bones. Heat immediately rose around them, along with the smell of diesel. And burning, rotting meat.

Pakol's scream died out, but he kept firing flames down the stairs every few seconds. Not a constant jet of flame, but bursts. The stench of burning flesh grew stronger.

Joe stepped back. Sameer took his place, firing his AK-47 down occasionally. The temperature of the place shot up, and everyone around Pakol was drenched in sweat.

Joe wiped his forehead. "Got maybe a few minutes," he said.

Jason nodded, fingering the detonator. "Got some C-4 outside. Going to blow it."

"When?" Joe asked.

Jason shrugged. "Probably a few minutes."

Joe barked out a laugh. Even Lilly rolled her eyes. They were all feeling it, the approach of death. And they all were ready.

"Need to get up top," Joe said.

Jason nodded. "Just trying to pull as many in as we can for the blast. With any luck we'll get this rakshasa guy."

Lilly fired down the stairs, past Sameer. The big man looked back and bobbed his head once. And smiled.

The blasts of heat coming back from the flamethrower grew unbearable. Jason took a step back. Joe did as well. Pakol still stood there, though, blisters on his face, his hands. Keeping up the bursts.

A flamethrower had maybe ninety seconds of continuous spray. The way Pakol was working it, a burst every few seconds, had given them a few minutes. But that was all they had, and Jason was sure Pakol would be running dry soon.

It was time to get up top. Hopefully the three Rangers up there had kept the roof clear. "It's time," Jason said.

"Shit," Lilly said, almost at the same time. She was looking over Jason's shoulder. He turned, and swore, too. The windows on the third floor were packed with scourges, pressing through the tiny squares.

The dead bodies, pressing in, three stories above the ground.

Three stories above the ground. There were just that many of them outside that the creatures had piled up high around the monastery. The scourge surrounding the building must have looked like an anthill. The bodies had pushed and climbed on each other until they piled high around them.

Shit, Jason thought. *If they get to the top before us, then we'll be trapped when it all blows.*

"Run!" he screamed.

At the same time, something grabbed Sameer's foot and yanked him down the stairs. Joe stepped forward and fired a few rounds below. Sameer's hand appeared. Lilly slid forward and tried to pull the big man up.

Jason saw Sameer's arm was on fire. It was molten-hot down there. Lilly grimaced and looked to the side, pulling on Sameer's arm with both hands.

Joe kept shooting. Pakol stood there, flamethrower pointed up, not sure what to do.

Sameer screamed, something loud and piercing. His hand pulled out of Lilly's. Then he was gone. Though his scream went on and on.

"Go!" Jason shouted, pulling Pakol back. Joe kept firing,.Lilly lay there, looking down, face pale and eyes open. As if she didn't want to see what she had seen.

Jason pulled a frag off his belt. *What the hell?* he thought, and pulled a third. His last. He pulled both pins and got ready to toss them down the stairs.

He froze for a minute. He wished he hadn't looked. Sameer lay there on the stairs, on fire, melting, bits of his body being torn apart, flesh hot enough to stretch in the black hands of the scourges. One gooey arm was being tugged away from the big man's body.

Joe fired, and Sameer's face exploded. "Fire in the hole," Joe said quietly, as if Jason holding two live grenades were a usual thing.

Jason shook himself. Tossed the grenades down. The first explosion was muffled, but the second one seemed to get more in the blast.

They all headed to the fourth floor. Pakol had dropped the flamethrower and the backpack. Lilly was in front, and stopped halfway.

Patrick was right above them. "Those things are at the top," the Ranger said, breathing heavily. "They are all around this place."

The Benelli sounded off above them. Jason shook his head. "Get to the top, people."

His team headed up. Pakol stood there, chest heaving, facing back down the stairs. The man looked exhausted. As if his whole life had led to this moment, and he just didn't have any energy left.

Jason grabbed Pakol, pulling him behind him. Where his whole team stood, staring up the last set of stairs.

Grimm was there, firing the Benelli. Suzy lay on the steps below him, eyes pressed tightly together, holding her arm. Her body armor was covered in liquid, whether it was the scourge's blood or hers, Jason couldn't tell. Joe grabbed Suzy and tossed her over his shoulder in a fire-man's carry.

Suzy screamed. More blood streamed down from her arm and puddled around the Italian's feet. Her hand gripped tight to one arm.

Lilly rushed past both of them, trying to cover Grimm. Bodies had started to press against them.

They had to get to the top, Jason thought. *It's our only chance.*

"Grimm!" Jason shouted. "Make a hole!"

The Ranger didn't give any sign of hearing Jason, but fired a few more times, then screamed and swung the shotgun wildly, pushing the press of bodies back step by step, forcing his way onto the roof. Grimm looked like a berserker. He moved almost too fast to see, and he made room for them on the roof by sheer will.

Lilly was right behind him. Firing her gun in erratic bursts. Patrick behind her, doing the same. Joe was next, with Suzy on his shoulders. Her eyes open, and not blinking.

Jason pushed that thought away, and dragged Pakol behind his team. The roof was a swarm of scourges. They flowed everywhere. The keening sound was everywhere. There was just a small semicircle around Grimm,

Lilly, and Patrick. Up close the scourges' bodies appeared long dead, their skin dry and torn in patches, muscles and fat long gone, just ligaments and tendons left, twitching as their limbs moved.

Jason's team circled the roof at the top of the stairs, everyone focused outward, emptying the last of their magazines. Jason pulled Pakol up the last step, shoving the man onto the roof. Then Jason grabbed the detonator, taking a last look.

Grimm had fallen to one knee. The scourge flowed over him. Lilly ran out of ammo. Patrick fell underneath the wave. Joe turned back to look at Jason, his eyebrow raised. Jason held the detonator up and put one thumb on the switch.

Pakol pushed past Jason. Walking backward, and staring down the stairs. As if he was still searching for Sameer. But the word he whispered wasn't the big man's.

"Zahir," Pakol said. His face a mix of sadness and fury. "Why?"

The little man had been nowhere around. Jason hadn't seen him at each floor. Hadn't even thought of Zahir. But he did now, and he realized, just like Pakol did, where the rakshasa had been.

Or who he had been.

Dammit.

Jason flipped the switch.

The C-4 exploded around them, one after the next, louder and louder, closer and closer. Until they got close enough to be right next to Jason, and blew the world apart.

CHAPTER FOUR

The stars sat overhead, blurry pinpricks of bright light in a moonless sky. Sulfur hung in the air, a thick rotten egg kind of smell, mixed with the light scent of dust. It was quiet all around, with only the ticking of tiny pebbles in the background, from still-settling rock and rubble that remained after the building had collapsed.

Jason looked around. Or tried. His head was stuck, a large, cold weight holding it on all sides. The weight and chill of unearthed stone.

He checked himself. Or tried. He had a hard time moving, and thought maybe something in his spine had broken, which freaked him out a bit. He finally realized he was buried in the stone, and all of it pressed down on him, keeping him from moving. A big slab of it lay across his chest, along with piles of smaller rocks where his arms might be, the result of the explosion.

Either Jason hadn't calculated correctly or some of the C-4 had made its way inside. Maybe the scourge had brought it in. Either way, the building had blown, and the roof had come down.

Literally.

Jason tried to work an arm or leg free, but nothing moved. Not even his fingers. And he couldn't move his head much. It felt pinched. The weight of the slab and all the rock around him felt like a heavy stone blanket. It wrapped him and kept him immobilized.

The ticking of the pebbles felt like a clock. He fought an urge to scream. There wasn't an easy way out, but at least no scourges were eating him. Jason felt like that was a plus. He blinked a few times, closing his eyes hard and opening them, again and again, until his eyesight cleared.

The night sky of the Hindu Kush was beautiful. Brilliantly lit with stars. On a night like tonight, Jason could almost see the wispy whiteness stretching across the sky, like an arm of the Milky Way.

"Joe?" he called out. His voice felt thin. Jason tried calling again, hearing the ticking of the pebble clock in the background, timing his calls for the empty moments between the sliding of the rocks. He changed the names up, trying Lilly, Patrick, Grimm. It felt like the calls went on a long time.

"Yo," the Italian finally answered. Somewhere above Jason's head, and behind him.

"You good?" Jason asked.

"Depends on the definition," the Italian said. "It feels like a thousand pounds of rock is on top of me."

"Same here," Jason said. "Those creatures?"

"Not moving," Joe confirmed.

"Anyone else make it?"

"Don't know," Joe said. "Lost Suzy when the building went up. But—"

Jason had seen her, at the end. Eyes open. "I know."

"Yeah," Joe said.

Another groan interrupted them. Like someone coming out of a deep sleep. Or an old man, trying to get out of a chair.

"Ice? Flower?" Jason called out. "Grimm?"

"Yeah," Grimm answered. His voice sounded as if he was still out of it.

"You okay?"

"Probably," he finally answered. "Feel like I've been hit by a truck. Then backed over. Then hit again."

"Can you move?" Jason asked. "Joe and I are stuck."

There was a grunt, and pebbles trickled over rock. "Maybe a hand. A finger. Something."

Jason breathed out a sigh of relief. "Can you get free?"

Another pebble or two. "Maybe," Grimm said. "Going to take some time."

"We got that," Jason said, staring back up at the night. The stars seemed exceptionally clear, tiny pinpoints of bright white light in a blue-black sky. The three of them were quiet. There wasn't much sound, except for Grimm, trying to work himself free.

"Anyone else make it?" Grimm asked, after a bit.

"Not sure," Jason said.

"Oh." There was a grunt, and another one, from the Ranger. Stones trickled and fell. "You know, Jason, I never did see that thing."

"Yeah," Jason said. "It wasn't out there. It was with us."

A bit of silence. "Which one?"

"There was a thin guy, with a ponytail," Jason said.

"In the building?" Grimm said.

"I thought he was there," Jason said. "One on of the floors. Never saw him after the fight started."

"Damn," Grimm said. There was the sound of his hand, or arm, moving. More pebbles sliding.

Time passed, Jason wasn't sure how long; there didn't seem to be a moon out. Just an occasional pant from Grimm as he worked. "It's heavy, Jason."

"Tell us about it," Joe said.

"Not sure if I can get free," Grimm said.

Jason tried pushing on the slab of stone holding him down. All he could feel was his shoulders bunch up. His arms seemed to be locked in. He pushed until he screamed with the effort.

"Grimm, it's got to be you," Jason said. "Because it's not going to be me."

Someone cursed then. Not Joe or Grimm. It was a swear Jason had heard a million times. *Lilly*.

"Flower," Jason called out, "that you?"

There was a long moment of silence. Even Grimm seemed to have stopped working out of the rock. "Yeah," she finally said.

"Hurt?" Jason asked.

"Not sure," Lilly said. "More mad that I missed my *Game Over* moment."

Grimm laughed. Jason grinned. Even Joe had a smile in his voice.

"Maybe next time we have a horde of zombies blow up around us," the Italian said.

"No kidding," Lilly said. "Who planted the C-4? That was all kinds of Charlie Foxtrot."

"Can you move?" Jason asked.

"Don't know," she said. "Can't feel much."

Hopefully she was just trapped, like the rest of them. Jason couldn't really feel anything himself, other than the large weight holding him down. A thought entered his head that scared him. Even if Grimm got out, he might not be able to free the rest of the team.

Jason quickly shoved that thought away. He put it next to wondering about Suzy and Patrick. It was a miracle that some of the team had survived, and Jason had to work the problem in front of them. Get as many as he could home.

Once Grimm was free, they could work the next problem. Then the next. All the way until Jason was home, and then he could start wondering about things like how he could have done better. He could start blaming himself for those who had died. He could wonder who sent them out here, who Pakol was, what the hell the scourge had been.

One step at a time.

There was the sound of rocks moving. The little clicks and clacks as Grimm worked himself free. "Might as well watch some *Ever After*, Lils," the Ranger said. "Since you got some time."

Lilly barked out a laugh, then groaned a bit. "Fuck you, Grimm. You know that's always been your movie."

Grimm laughed. It sounded strange from the man. It wasn't a sound he usually made. The name Grimm had stuck for a reason.

"You know," Grimm said, "that's not the kind of thing you should say to the person who's going to dig you out."

"I shouldn't say it," Lilly replied, "but if admitting I like that movie is the price of getting out of here, then you might as well leave me."

Grimm laughed again. Even Jason grinned.

"You guys should watch real movies," Joe said.

"What," Lilly asked, "like *Casino*? *Donnie Brasco*? *Goodfellas*?"

"Hey," Joe replied, "don't argue with the classics."

"I'm gonna make you an offer you can't refuse," Grimm said, in some weird gravelly accent.

Everyone stopped talking.

"Was that your *Godfather* impression?" Lilly finally asked. "Because it's flat-out horrible."

Grimm let out a big sigh but kept on with the accent. "I respect those that tell me the truth, no matter how hard it is."

Then the Ranger kept working. Each tick of a pebble felt like the hour hand of a clock. His progress was slow. Jason could hear him grunt and groan with exertion. And Grimm just had one hand free.

Lilly and Joe talked movies for a bit. Jason joined in. Grimm, too, when he was taking a breather. The conversation went from talking about old mobster movies, to some of the newer *Star Wars* flicks, to what show they wanted to see when they got back.

Going overseas was weird like that. The world back home changed so much in the six months they were gone. There was always an adjustment. And if they were gone longer, a year or two, who knew what movies had come out in that time? What music had changed? Jason remembered coming home once and his favorite rock station had become country.

At some point Grimm let out a big exhale. "Arm free."

"Huzzah," Lilly said, in a tone that helped Jason imagine her rolling her eyes. "At this rate, we'll be free right after the war ends."

Grimm laughed, then groaned.

"You good, Grimm?" Jason asked.

"Broken ribs," Grimm said, his words short. "Working through it."

They all fell quiet after that. Talked out, maybe. After a bit someone started snoring. *Joe*. Jason shook his head. The Italian could always nap.

"It sure is cold," Lilly remarked once.

Grimm grunted, maybe an assent, maybe still working his way out. They were all sitting, waiting, and Jason had no idea if Grimm could even get free, much less dig out the rest of the team. The slab of rock on Jason's chest could be more than anyone could lift. He might die here. They all still might die here.

One problem at a time, Jason thought. He focused on his breathing. Long draw, long exhale. Rinse and repeat. He tried to relax and listen to the rhythm of Grimm working, of rocks ticking over rocks. Then he tried to follow Joe's idea and sleep, but that eluded him as well. There was a sense inside Jason, a worry, an unease, that kept him awake and listening to Grimm. Something telling him it wasn't over.

"Just my legs now," Grimm finally said.

"Take your sweet time, Grimm," Lilly called out.

"I'm hurrying," Grimm argued. His breath short.

"Sounds like it," Lilly said. "I hear the same thing in PT every morning. Some guy panting waaaayyyy behind me."

"Ha," Grimm said.

The two went back to mocking each other. The way brothers and sisters do. Jason knew what Lilly was doing. Distracting Grimm from the pain. Distracting everyone from their worry. Grimm was their only hope. He knew it. They knew it.

It had been a long time since Jason had eaten. He wondered when his stomach would rumble. Or when he would get thirsty.

"Almost out," Grimm said, finally. Then, "Huh." There was a tinging sound of metal against rock, then a long metallic scraping sound.

Then a voice burst out. Not Joe or Lilly or Grimm. It was panicked. *"What the fuck?"*

The three of them listened, but there was nothing else.

Joe had woken. "Was that Ice?"

Still nothing but silence.

"Sounded like him," Lilly said.

"Patrick?" Jason asked. Quietly.

No one answered. Jason heard the scraping sound, over by Grimm. Then a large groan. A heaving sound. Then a rumble of rubble as a heavy rock slid slowly across a face of stone.

"Free," Grimm said. "Might see Ice. See a foot, at least."

Jason heard Grimm's combat boots strike pebbles, as if he was walking on gravel.

Grimm cursed.

"Grimm?" Lilly asked.

Someone threw up, a big heaving sound, repeating itself a couple times. "One sec," Grimm answered, his voice thick.

Jason waited, not liking the feel of what was happening.

"Ice didn't make it," Grimm finally said. His voice a little shaky.

Teams always were a brotherhood, a family. They were as close as anyone could be. Losing one person was always a gut punch. It would feel like missing a limb for the longest time. But losing Ice and Q? Two would take some time. Something Jason could beat himself up with later.

This problem now.

"Where you at, Flower?" Grimm asked.

"Oh, I'm next?" Lilly asked. Jason heard her trying to keep her voice upbeat.

"Wanted to give you one last chance," Grimm replied, with something like a smile in his voice. Like he was forcing himself to find some cheer, too. "What's your favorite movie?"

"Guess I'm not going anywhere," Lilly said. "At least, not until—"

Then she stopped talking. "Lilly?" Grimm asked. He spoke again, his voice intense. *"Flower?"*

Grimm threw up again, retching sounds from deep inside him. Dry, heaving sounds. Then Grimm spoke, the Ranger's voice low. Guttural, even. *"Fuck.* Fuck this. Fuck it all."

"Grimm?" Jason called. "Is Lilly okay?"

"Fuck," Grimm screamed, over where Lilly's voice had been. The word echoed up the hill and bounced off the cliffs, reverberating to them.

"Joe?" Jason asked, feeling lost. Not understanding what was going on. The Italian didn't answer, even though Grimm walked by where Joe had been.

"Coming, Jason," Grimm said. His voice sounded resigned. More of the combat-boots-on-gravel sound. Pebbles, shifting and sliding at every step. A shadow moved across Jason's vision from his left, blotting out the bright stars above.

"Thank God, man," Jason said, seeing Grimm. "Is Lilly okay? Joe?"

The shadow grew until the Ranger stood above him. In one hand he still held the Benelli. Grimm's vest was dirty and dusty, covered in a little blood and a lot of vomit. His eyes blurry and wet and unfocused.

"Help me out, man," Jason told him.

Grimm leaned over and picked up something, holding it loosely in his hand. It was a hand, and part of a forearm, torn apart where the arm would usually meet an elbow. Bright white bone protruded from that end, dripping blood. On the other end, fingers wrapped tightly around a detonator.

The Ranger looked down at Jason. Grimm's face was almost expressionless, as if the man was placing all his emotions behind a big wall. Still, a sadness remained. Tears ran from the Ranger's eyes, leaving muddy trails down his face.

"I don't understand," Jason said. The weight on his chest grew heavier. Colder. Frigid.

Grimm just shook his head. "I'm sorry, Jason." The stars behind the Ranger grew brighter in the night sky, like they were coming closer.

"Tell me, Grimm," Jason said. "Help me understand."

Grimm stood above Jason, the stars swelling behind him. The weight on Jason's chest grew heavier and heavier. Grimm was saying something, but Jason could no longer hear him. A ringing, like bells maybe, had taken over. Something he hadn't noticed before, but the sound had grown loud in his ears.

The stars grew brighter and brighter. Like they were coming at him at a thousand miles per hour. Until it was everything Jason could see. Until everything in his vision was a bright white, all other visions consumed by the light, and nothing else remained.

CHAPTER FIVE

A gray light rose in the east, just a tiny sliver of dawn. It was a new day, one none of my friends would see. Only me and the dead. My team and mixed in with all the rubble the hundreds, if not thousands of old broken bodies of the scourge. There was a leg, pointing straight up. Dark rags, torn and ripped among the rubble. Part of a face, peeking out from under the rock.

I finally tossed Jason's arm. I don't know why I did. The limb fell to the side of Jason, whose chest had been crushed by a huge slab of what looked like limestone. His head nestled among the stones, and blood soaking the area around him. Eyes wide-open, unblinking.

Dead. Like his entire team.

Help me understand, his ghost had asked.

How the fuck could I do that? I thought. *When I don't understand? These ghosts, my friends, why could I see them? Why did they hang around?*

I looked up into the night, taking a deep breath. *Why let them talk to me?*

All of them were dead. Torn apart in the explosion. For some reason, I had survived the blast. Even though the whole building had come down around us.

A brief moment flashed into my head. Suzy, standing behind me on the stairs. Pushing me up onto the roof, in the middle of the scourge.

Even though I had left her lying on the steps. Thinking she was already dead.

The memory was clearer now. Sharper. Jason had shouted to make a hole. Suzy had been behind me, in front of Lilly. I had felt Q's hands on my back, pushing me up. I had felt stronger, faster. A burst of energy rushed through me, from Suzy. Like I had drunk a thousand cups of coffee. Electricity surged through my limbs, and all of a sudden I could push through the scourges, beat them down, break their bodies, tear off their skulls.

The energy swelled into me, from Suzy. I had fought onto the roof. Thinking maybe I could fight our way out. The night was still dark all around us. The scourges swelled over me like a black wave, and I threw them back and took another step. Lilly and Patrick shooting the creatures around me. I screamed and swung and worked my way forward, a step at a time, away from the stairs.

If Jason wanted a hole, I would damn well make one.

Then the energy had left me. So fast, like it never had existed. There was a flash of Suzy, rushing through my mind …

I was in a kitchen, a tiny square thing, with yellowed tile on the floor, and on old white stove. A big bowl sat on the counter by the stove, and a flat metal pan on the top of the oven.

A small table next to me, with a plate of cookies on it. The plate was white and round, and the cookies were a sugary tan, with dark lumps of chocolate in them. I smiled and inhaled the warm scents of cake and cocoa.

A woman walked to the oven. Old, with gray hair tied behind her head in a bun. Thick glasses on her face, an old, stained apron wrapped around her midsection. I didn't recognize her, and yet at the same time I knew this woman was Suzy's mother. The woman turned back a little, one large wooden spoon in her hand, thick batter stuck lumped at the end of the spoon, and with her other hand patted Suzy's head, absently. My head.

I was Suzy.

Suzy laughed. She (we) reached a tiny hand out and grabbed another cookie from the plate. Cookies, soft and warm, straight from an oven.

They melted in our mouth, sugar and chocolate warm on top of our tongue, the bits of chocolate soft and gooey.

Somehow I was living a memory of Suzy's. I couldn't move her, but I was along for this ride. I felt how happy Suzy was in that moment. How warm. How content. She and her mother, baking cookies before the holidays. Waiting on Dad to come home.

"Take as many as you need, Suze," her mother told her. Me. Us. "Just remember to leave some for your brother ..."

A moment later I was back on the rooftop, surrounded by the scourge, in the middle of the night. The air thick with sweat, with musty clothes and rotting meat, with the metallic scent of shots being fired, of sulfur. Lilly and Patrick, to my right and left.

I was screaming.

No time had passed, even though it felt like I had been in that memory for minutes. The shock of the transition surprised me, and I fell to one knee. I realized the burst of energy I had was leaving me. I tried to hold on to it, tried to somehow pull it all into me. I needed to keep making a hole. I needed to take another step. I screamed and pushed against the scourge swarming over me.

Jason must have blown the C-4 then. The explosion had torn the monastery down. Our group had been tossed in the air, a lot of weight had pushed in on me, and I had huddled up, trying to resist it.

Then darkness.

Then I had woken.

And now I was standing here, above all the bodies of those who had been with me. Every single one of them dead.

It was Danny, all over again.

Just on the other side of the world.

Some time later I started moving. The monastery had sunk inward in the explosion, leaving a large pile of rock and rubble. We were still high up off the ground.

Maybe it was time to give up, I thought. *I can't seem to outrun this. No matter where I go, people die.*

No matter how hard I searched. No matter where I went. No matter how hard I tried to always be first, I was always the last one left. My throat was raw from screaming, though my body felt okay, oddly enough.

It didn't seem right, or fair. But when had life ever been fair, for me? *To* me?

All I leave is ghosts.

I wasn't that careful walking down. I fell a couple of times. When I did, I stayed down for long moments before getting back up. Emotionally I was in some dead zone, feeling nothing.

Patrick's shotgun fell out of my hand, tumbled down the slope before me. I stared at it, far below me, at the bottom of a landslide of rubble, before deciding to get it. It seemed small, but I had told him I'd take care of it. I tripped over a slab getting there and landed badly on my side. A burst of pain shot through me from my ribs.

That pain woke me a bit, though. I kept struggling on. Unsure of the reason why. Maybe it was just being human. Moving, when all seemed lost. Going on, after everything had been taken from you.

I got to the bottom of the rubble when I noticed the bloodstains. A trail, like someone had been dragged. It led a few feet down the street, then turned sharply into one of the buildings. One that remained somewhat standing. At least, two of its walls still stood, though the roof was gone. The stains led in through a doorway.

Voices came from the doorway.

I moved along, not meaning to be quiet, but taking small, staggered steps. Until I was in the doorway, leaning against one side of it, watching. For some reason, captivated. As if this was something I was meant to see.

The man in the pakol cap lay off to the side. His legs both broken, his pants soaked in blood. His face was blistered and burned, and one eye was swollen shut. A trail of blood led to the man, from where he had been dragged along the ground.

A thin man crouched in front of him, with long hair tied back in a ponytail. The thin man was covered in dust, but otherwise looked healthy. Like he hadn't even been in the building when the C-4 went up.

Pakol laughed. It was an ugly, gurgling thing. He spat out blood. "You were our brother," he said.

"This body has not been your brother for some time," the thin man said. The guy with the ponytail.

The thin man had a short, curved knife in one hand. He took that and pushed it into one of Pakol's legs. Pakol screamed, but not loudly, and ended in a wheeze. As if he didn't have a lot of air left.

The thin man pulled out the knife, and then he laughed. The rakshasa. The thing. I blinked and saw and felt the dark evil I had felt the day before. If I had seen him then, I could have saved my friends. I could have saved everyone.

"You humans," the rakshasa said, "with your connections. Your family. Your friends. Your *brothers*. Always a weakness."

"What happened to Zahir?" Pakol gasped.

"What happened?" The thin man tapped the blade on his chin, the knife leaving a bloody dot there. "What always happens with humans. They see the inevitable, and then they give up."

"I should have seen it," Pakol said.

"Of course you should have," the rakshasa said. "All your friends dying. All your family. All the people killed around you. It was only a matter of time before your friend gave up. Gave in.

"After all," the creature said, "you all *want* to live."

Then another plunge of the knife into the leg. Another scream from Pakol. Another tug of the blade out, accompanied by a wet sound.

"Do you even know why," Pakol gasped, "you don't finish me?"

"I do," the rakshasa said. "This is the best part."

He leaned over, taking a deep breath above Pakol. "The fear, the pain, it is a fuel for my kind."

Pakol spat more blood out. His face twisted in a grimace. "It is not that."

"No?" The rakshasa punched his knife back into Pakol's leg. Grinning at the scream. "Enlighten me."

Pakol gasped and wheezed and spat out more blood. His eyes rolled back in his head. His moan became a gurgle.

The rakshasa pulled out his knife, and waited.

Pakol took a long breath, then let it go. His face relaxed, as if he no longer could feel pain. "It is only because he isn't here."

"He?" The rakshasa tilted his head. "The only other man is trapped above, in the rock. I saw it myself, before gathering you."

The creature looked sad, as if he was enjoying what he was doing, but knew the time for playing around was growing short. "It is probably time I got to him."

The Benelli was in my hands. I pulled the trigger. There was a boom, a splatter of blood over the wall, and the rakshasa pitched over. I stood over him and fired a couple more times, until his head became a mist against the rock. And then the Benelli went empty.

I kicked the thing then, making sure it was dead.

"Get to this, you fuck," I said, aloud. I wasn't angry when I said the words. I was in a land past anger. A cold place where everything I wanted to feel couldn't reach me. The despair and the hate and the rage pounded outside, knocked on the door, trying to get in.

I turned back to the man in the pakol cap. He lay there, his chest rising and falling, taking large, deep breaths, his face at peace. As if his legs weren't shattered underneath him, his face burned and blistered.

"So," he said, "you are he."

"Me?" I asked. "I am what?"

One arm went to his chest. It pulled something out from underneath his shirt. A stone on a string. He had a hard time working the rope out from behind his neck, so I knelt and helped him.

Close up the stone looked old. It was smaller than my hand, maybe the size of my palm, and round. Like a cookie, I thought, pushing down a manic giggle.

Three concentric rings lay on its surface, each ring inside the other. Between the rings lay shapes, etchings in the stone. They almost looked hieroglyphic, a puzzle, and I felt if I could spin the rings a bit the shapes would line up and all make sense.

"Take it," Pakol said.

I did not reach out for it. The stone felt old. There was a power in it. I thought about looking at it, like I did when I looked for colors. The ghost-like vision I had. But I was scared to.

"Take it," he said again.

I did not want any part of that stone.

"Listen," Pakol said. His words coming out hard, in short sentences, like he was pushing them out of his chest. "Solomon's Key. Keep. From demon."

"Didn't I just kill the demon?" I looked at the thin man next to us, unmoving.

Pakol shook his head. "He was." He took another long breath. "Trick." Then he tried again. "Trap."

"Is this what all this was about?" I asked, waving my hands around. "Why my friends are all dead?"

The man's eyes were full of pain, and sadness. Something happened to him, and his body relaxed. As if he had passed some threshold of pain, and he could no longer feel the agony he was in. His voice was steadier, though he spoke in a near whisper. "Better this. Better your friends than the world."

He pushed the stone toward me. The Key, whatever he called it. I kept my hands from him, and he groaned, frustrated. "Never hand it to him."

"I don't understand," I said.

"This stone holds his brothers and sisters," he tried to explain. "If they are freed, the world suffers."

His eyes rolled up in the back of his head, and his body shook for a long, long moment. The entire time he remained silent. Enduring. Then went limp.

Then his chest shuddered. He took a long, long breath. As if willing himself to stay alive. His eyes remained tightly pressed together. His hand trembled, holding the Key out to me.

I could maybe believe in demons. Especially after today. I had seen things in my past that had me believing Evil, with a capital *E*, was a real thing. But this stone, this man, my friends, this scourge, it all didn't add up to anything I liked.

I shook my head, then said quietly, "No."

The man smiled. His eyes remained shut. He said, still whispering, "If you want the deaths of your friends to mean something, then take this. Keep it."

Where you at, Flower?

I didn't think I would ever be rid of that moment. Walking up to Lilly, getting ready to dig her out from under the rubble. Us joking together.

It had been a long time since I had someone I could lean on, years after Jen. It was nice to have someone treat you like part of the family. To be a part of something. Lilly had been like a sister to me. *Wanted to give you one last chance ...*

Then I had found her ghost, lying on bloodstained rubble. Her body lying on top of all the rocks, just her skull gone. Sitting in its place had been a large stone, as if it had fallen on Lilly while she was lying there, and crushed it. One eye dangled in the space between the rock and where her face had been. A jumble of tiny white blocks underneath. Teeth. And a puddle of red tissue.

That was all I could see of my friend. I let out a shaky breath. My last memory of Lilly shouldn't be this.

Her ghost had been responding to me, likely getting ready to rag me some more. Then her spirit became confused, it lost focus, and then …

Then it disappeared.

My jaw set. A whirlwind of emotion ran through me, from the dead zone I had been living in. It burst through the wall I had built. The raw, angry winds blew the barrier down and whipped through me. Whatever creature wanted this, if it was responsible for what had happened to my friends, then the least I could do was keep this stone from him.

It would give my life some meaning.

So I tugged the rope out of his hands. When I did, a large breath left him, like the dying winds of a storm long in the making, as it passed over the horizon.

"Thank you, my friend," he said. "Thank you."

Then he died.

His eyes remain closed. He shuddered once and went slack with a long, wheezing breath that died into a low moan. He was covered in burns, skin bubbled and blistered, his legs lying broken, smashed, at different angles.

I shuddered a little. I hadn't known him, but it was a hard death. One a man ought not to have to go through, but maybe one I would have to prepare for. I stared at the body, taking it in. The broken bones, shattered legs, the thick red blood soaking the ground around him.

If I was this new keeper of the Key, and a demon wanted to take this stone from me, there was a good chance I would face this same fate.

I felt like I deserved it. People died just for knowing me. Friends were killed just because I was around them. Maybe this Key was a penance, something I needed to do, in order to pay off those debts.

The stone was lighter than I thought. Each concentric circle was perfect, one circle inside the other. Each circle had seven quadrants, and different marks lay in each one, like stick figure drawings. Or early Egyptian, or something. I wasn't a history guy.

Each stone fit tightly against the next, but they spun easily, as if they were well oiled. Spinning them around, I discovered different shapes as the segments lined up. Sometimes the picture almost made sense. Maybe this was the original Rubik's cube. What had the man called it?

Solomon's Key? I placed the rope around my neck and tucked the Key into my shirt. It was a spot of coolness against my skin.

I stayed kneeling next to the dead man for a long time. The sun began its rise in the east, and a gray daylight dropping down over us like a curtain, washing the shadows away. For the first time I felt cold, really cold from the night, as the rays of the sun lit upon my skin, carrying the tiniest bit of warmth.

I thought about the green color I had seen, flickering in his chest. It was a shade I had never seen before, and I wondered what it meant. Obviously it wasn't something I could ask now. I would have to figure out more about myself, and more about the stone, if I was going to avoid the fate of the man before me.

And the fate of my friends. They were all gone. They had died bad deaths as well, apparently because of this Key. Because a demon had chased this man to this monastery, and we had been here to meet him. Lilly. Jason. Joe. Patrick. Suzy.

Suzy's ghost. Thinking about that brought the final moments in the monastery back. Her spirit had some kind of energy, and she had pushed all of that into me. Enough so that I had gone into some kind of berserker mode. I had made it to the roof. And somehow I had used that energy to survive the blast, when no one else in my team had.

It was the only way I could have survived.

Flashes of memories came to me, from after the explosion. Of being tossed in the air with a million pounds of stone, of the press of boulders sandwiching my body, of a bunch of my ribs cracking. I remembered balling up and trying to resist the weight as it smashed against me.

And I had resisted that weight. Nothing had crushed me. And I found, lightly pressing my hand against my side, fewer ribs were broken than I had thought. As if they had healed.

I had always just seen ghosts. Tonight I had lived a memory of one. And I had used the energy that spirit was tied to. It was an act I had never done before, a power I was unaware I had, and it had saved me. But it also scared me.

What was I?

I didn't know. Maybe cursed.

CHAPTER SIX

The gray light of predawn lightened into a brilliant blue of morning. Birds chirped from above. Maybe real Afghan snowfinches. For them the day began anew, no matter all the dead people below. The scourge. The explosions. For them the sun brought about a reset. Another day, possibly different from the last. Possibly the same.

For my team, my friends, the dead man in front of me, they were forever stuck in yesterday. My knee hurt. I had been kneeling a long time. I didn't know if it was because I had no idea what to do next, or didn't have any energy to do anything.

I didn't think I could go back to the base. Something told me they would never believe this story. Or why I was the only person to make it back.

"Azir, Azir, Azir," a voice came from behind me, a confident voice. "Look at where you ended up."

I spun around, the Benelli rock-steady in my grip. A man stood behind me, in the same doorway I had entered. He wore a nice suit, one apparently tailored to fit. A pale white jacket and pants, with black pinstripes, a black shirt, open at the collar. His shoes had a nice luster, as if he hadn't walked through a million pounds of rubble to get here.

Somewhere above us both, an Afghan finch warbled again. Or whistled. Whatever. It had been a long night. I pulled the trigger.

The Benelli clicked, empty.

I tried again. And got the same result. The same snap of the hammer on an empty chamber.

"Looky there," he said, grinning. "Shoot first, ask questions later?"

He squatted down, putting his eyes level with mine. The irises were black, and seemed to vibrate slightly. The feel of his stare unnerved me. "As a general policy, that's not normally something I'm interested in. I'm more of a guy who likes to appreciate his situation, take the measure of a man before me, before I start killing."

His teeth, too, were perfect. Too straight. Too … pearly white.

"You're the demon," I said.

He cocked his head and laughed. "Oh, we got a bright one." He reached an open hand past the Benelli. "Azazel."

I leaned away from him. My knee screamed at me to stand, and part of me was afraid to. Standing would mean running, and if this was the demon, I didn't want to start that now.

If this was the demon, maybe I wouldn't have to. Maybe I could fight, instead. End this all now. Take revenge for my friends. I still had my nine-millimeter, though I would have to either drop the shotgun or draw it cross-handed. And I had my knife.

After holding his hand out a minute, Azazel pulled it back.

"You're the one responsible," I said.

Azazel looked around. "For all of this?" He shook his head. "I didn't *do* any of this. I don't have to. Men do enough on their own."

"For their deaths," I explained.

"For Azir?" he asked. "His friends? Your recon team? I killed none of them."

"You didn't send these things?" I moved the shotgun so that it pointed to the thin man. "The rakshasa?"

"Well, I'll confess there." Azazel grinned again. It was something he apparently enjoyed doing, and it felt cocky to me. "I didn't *not* send them."

"Then you are responsible," I said, and carefully dropped the shotgun.

The demon stood. "I guess if you want to blame someone, you could blame me."

"It's good enough for me," I said, and in a swift motion pulled out my nine-millimeter, emptying the magazine. The snap of each shot, all eighteen of them, felt good.

Azazel never moved. Each shot tore through him. Holes appeared in his chest, dark holes in a black shirt. His suit fluttered at every bullet.

He waited, cocking his eyebrow at me. Then he leaned forward a little, continuing our conversation. "But blame is like a river, right? It flows along, and no matter how you swim up it, there is always more. You can blame me. I can blame someone else, and on and on we go."

I started to worry then. I had seen things, killed things, that weren't human. The scourge was the latest thing I had encountered. In the beginning, it was just one vampire. But I had seen other undead since. Most of them would have at least been hurt by bullets.

The bullets I fired hadn't hurt him. And as I watched, the holes on his front closed in on themselves. The edges of his skin pressed tightly together, until all of a sudden it was whole.

Maybe I needed to play his game. I holstered the gun, as if I had never pulled the trigger.

"Every river has an origin," I said.

The demon's eyes widened. "Exactly, McNulty." He pointed at me. "Exactly."

"So you're saying I can blame you," I said, "but you can blame someone else?"

"Every river has an origin," he repeated.

"Sounds a little hypocritical," I said. "Maybe you just like passing the buck."

"Ha," Azazel snorted. "I think I'm going to like you, McNulty. You and I are going to have some fun."

"Only if you like dying," I said. "Because I'm going to kill you for this."

Azazel waved his finger in a *no* motion. "Hold on. You haven't heard the rules."

"What rules?"

"Of the game," Azazel said. "I think I call it *Key*paway. Get it?"

I shook my head at the bad pun. "I got it."

"Then let me give you a little advice." Azazel's voice grew low. Hoarse. "Give it to me. Now."

I wasn't sure I was going to live, but I was sure I wasn't giving the demon the Key. My friends deserved better. I beckoned the demon closer, and he leaned in.

"If I did that, then you couldn't call the game Keypaway," I told him, in a near whisper.

There was a long moment of silence between us. His voice was still low. "You and I, we are definitely going to have some fun."

"Whatever," I said.

"Do you know what the Key is?" he asked.

"Does it matter?" I asked.

"The appreciation of a thing always matters, Grimm," the demon said. He stood, and all of a sudden a cigarette appeared between his fingers. Lit. He took a puff and let out a breath of smoke, and the small cloud formed a tiny circle. Like the Key. "Always."

The cloud spun in a small circle, then disappeared.

"All I know is it holds your brothers and sisters," I said. "And if you want them, you'll have to go through my dead body."

"Oh," Azazel said, "like this guy?"

The demon picked up Azir by his leg, using one hand. Azazel shook the body, like he was wringing it out, and then tossed it aside. Azir's body hit a wall and plopped to the floor, arms and legs jumbled all together. Blood spattered everywhere.

Azazel looked at me, one eyebrow raised, the corner of his lip turned up slightly. Blood all over him. Then the demon shook his hand, and more drops of blood dotted the floor, Azazel's. His face looked like one of those Rorschach images.

Mine must have looked the same way. I stood and wiped my face, feeling the smear of liquid across it. My jaw set, my hand tight on the trigger of the empty shotgun.

"Just so we're clear," the demon told me.

I shook my head. Whatever this thing was, he delighted in pain. And he wanted to show that to me, *excessively* show it to me. "We're clear," I said.

"All you have to do is hand it over to me, you know," Azazel said. "Give it to me of your own free will, McNulty, and just walk away."

He shrugged. "I might even throw in a few things. Something to get out of here? Money? Whatever you need. Avoid all this pain coming your way. Because I love it. I'll bring it. And in the end, you'll be like Azir.

Broken. Everyone you know gone. Another worthless life spent, trying to keep my family from me."

A cool presence came into being next to me. Azir, or his ghost. His spirit stood above his body, his legs hanging underneath him, shattered and broken. The ghost translucent in the morning sun.

I wasn't sure how old the Key was, when it had been made, but it felt *old*. Thousands of years old. If that was the case, if there had been Keepers running with the Key that whole time, then there was a reason Azazel didn't have it yet.

"If it's that easy," I asked, "why don't you have it already?"

"Why?" Azazel looked up into the sky, like he was deep in thought. I wasn't sure if he was pretending to think, or actually doing it. "You might be thinking each of these Keepers held out long enough to pass the Key on," he said, and his smile turned dark. His eyes flashed. "But let me present you with another theory. Maybe I just like this game too much. Maybe it's a bit of fun for me."

Azir's spirit reached out to me, with one arm. Somehow it recognized me, much like Suzy had. His face was the most solid thing about him. His eyes flickered to Azazel, back to me. Back to the demon. As he stood there his spirit grew more solid, became a brighter blue, so bright I was surprised the demon didn't see him.

"If that's the case," I told the demon, "then you're going to be in a long line of people I've disappointed."

The demon cocked his head. I felt his gaze dig beneath me. Probing under my skin, searching. "There's something different about you, McNulty," he murmured, as if to himself. "Something I think I'm going to enjoy."

I wondered—if I looked myself in the mirror, with my colored sight,would I see green flicker in my chest? Or would it be something else? Was I different from Azir, from who had carried this Key before me?

I was different from anyone else I had met. No one could see ghosts, not that I knew. And I had never heard of anyone using energy from the spirits. I needed to learn more about myself, what I could do. Especially if I was going to keep this Key. If I was going to make this demon pay for what he had done to Lilly, Jason, Joe, Patrick, and Suzy.

If there was something I could do well, it was make people pay a price. My team was just the latest example in a long line of them. If I hadn't been a part of Recon Team, then they all would still be alive. If I hadn't been friends with Danny, he would still be, too.

So I would make this demon pay something more than he wanted. If it was the last thing I did. It was something I was good at.

The ghost of Azir put his hand on my shoulder. There was a thrumming between us, like the slight vibration in the air, something you could almost feel, when you stood beside a high-voltage transformer. The thrumming of a lot of electrical current.

I reached out into the spirit, with all my senses, trying to figure it out. Somewhere deep inside him was a ball of energy. The same energy Suzy's ghost had had.

I smiled. I wasn't sure what I was, but I was sure that I *was* different. In a way the demon might not like.

"You might enjoy it," I said, pulling out my knife. Smiling. "But then again, you might not."

The demon shook his head at me. "McNulty," Azazel said, drawing the word out, as if disappointed. He waved his hand to the bullet holes in his suit. "Didn't we already do this?"

Bullets didn't hurt him. Maybe the demon needed something a little more biblical. A little more medieval.

"The name," I told him, "is Grimm."

I took the energy from the ghost of Azir and jumped the demon. As soon as I touched the ball of power inside the ghost, a vitality shot through me. A force ratcheted up every muscle I had to eleven.

Just like when Suzy had done it earlier. Azazel grabbed at me, but I easily avoided his hands and landed on him. We both fell backward to the floor, and then I planted the KA-BAR knife right in the top of his head.

The hilt *thunked* against his skull. The demon froze. I picked him up and tossed him into the same wall he had thrown Azir into. Actually I tossed him *through* the wall. The stone exploded as Azazel went through it. The wall itself collapsed. Bits of rock bounced around, and a cloud of dust rolled outward, masking everything for a brief moment.

Then silence. Beams of sunlight broke through the dust. I blinked and wiped at my eyes. I was breathing hard, chest heaving in and out, energy coursing through my veins, my muscles, twitching along my nerves.

I looked over at where Azir's spirit was, using the vision I used to see the flickers of color inside people. Energy flowed out of the ghost and streamed toward me. The stream colored the cloud of dust between us, like a strobe of light did at a rave.

The energy I took seemed to be balled up inside the spirit, as if it was the end of a rope, tied together in a knot, stuck in a funnel. Almost like a tap. The energy stretched down through the funnel and reached from the spirit to slide into the ground, like the thick ropy power tethered him to some plane. The mouth of the funnel was open, and energy flowed from the ghost and into me. The flow looked almost ethereal, millions of tiny blue-white wisps channeled between us, tying us together.

Azir himself stood still. He faced me, his face sad, his eyes focus. Determined. Waiting. The cloud of dust blew out from us and washed away, leaving bright sunlight to illuminate the broken home. Under that sun, Azir began to fade away. The deep navy-white color of the spirit became a pale white, like a thinning cloud stretched across a deep blue sky.

Then there was laughter. Hard chuckles that broke the silence. Azazel's head popped over the broken wall. His suit was torn and covered in jagged pieces of rock. The knife still poked out of his skull, like a particularly bad haircut.

The demon reached up and yanked it out. A dark jet of fluid spurted briefly from his head. As dirty as Azazel was, his smile was still pearly white.

"I *am* going to enjoy this," he said, almost in wonder, as if the demon himself was surprised.

Then he jumped over the wall. I leaped to meet him. We collided in midair and landed in the middle of the broken building.

It was a street fight. I was still sped up. I moved as quick as lightning, but now Azazel moved just as fast as me. Both of our punches, when we hit, cracked and broke bone. We rolled around the rubble, exchanging head butts, punching, kicking. There was a pain in my side, and I realized my knife was stuck there, up to the hilt.

Though the pain was distant enough, I could ignore it and keep fighting. I tugged on the stream of ethereal energy, felt the force of it roll into me. Every time Azazel connected and broke something, a cool flow of power concentrated there and healed me.

We struggled and fought. My bones broke and reknit. Muscle tore and stitched itself back together, often in the middle of a punch. Slices of skin were scraped off on the rocks, and somehow regrew.

Azazel took his licks, too. I had landed plenty. His forehead was split in half, and a dark ichor leaked from the cut, the fluid smelling like sulfur. It had dripped into one of his eyes and colored it a solid black.

We wrestled around. I ended up on the bottom. Rocks dug into my back. The demon snarled, and seemed to gather himself. A knee planted in my stomach and the force of the blow popped something inside me. A hot, burning wetness spread through my belly, moving into my chest.

I spat out blood. The cool, healing pain inside me met the hot wetness, and seemed to hold it. I kept pulling more and more from Azir's ghost. His stream felt thinner to me of a sudden.

I realized I was moving slower than just a few seconds ago. Or the demon was moving faster. I swung and landed less, he swung back and connected. I rolled and held my arms over my chest, my face, trying to protect them. Azazel shoved my arms aside and started really throwing hard, swinging wildly.

I bucked him off and tried to crawl up the rubble. The stream of energy had become so thin it appeared like a tiny string, bobbing in the air between me and Azir. When I pulled the energy, it resisted me somehow.

"Where you going, *Grimm*?" Azazel asked. His feet crunched up the rubble behind me. Then two hands picked me up and slammed me back down into the rock.

Pain burst through me. I reached for Azir …

And three men sat by a fire. Azir. His big friend, and the thin man that I had just killed. Their names were Sameer and Zahir, and all of them were much, much younger. A small pot hung over the fire, and the thin man pulled out a spoon and tasted what was in it, before spitting to the side.

The three of them laughed. The night was big and empty above them. They talked, and wondered about their futures. Azir held the Key in his hand, the stone dangling on its rope from his hand, and Azir spun it. His friend said something, and Azir laughed …

What was I seeing there?

Then Azazel slammed me into the floor again. My head bounced off the rock, and I almost lost consciousness.

Azir in a city, walking fast, pushing the crowd of people around him.

The Key cool against his chest. His right arm held against his chest. It bled heavily, soaking through his sleeves. He was in a large market, full of robed people wearing turbans. Everyone wore different colors, stood at stalls, calling out their wares.

Azir yelled at them all. Screamed at them to run, even as he stumbled from stall to stall. Blood dripped off his arm and left large red puddles on the stones he staggered upon. Azir looked for something he could bind it with. There, a tailor's shop. He grabbed a length of cloth and wound it, over and over, around his arm.

The shopkeeper yelled at him, motioning to the purse hanging from his robed belt. The man called him a thief. Azir yelled back, telling the man to flee.

And then, in the background, the screams began ...

Azir's memories. I was seeing them, like Suzy's. I didn't understand why. I shook my head just as Azazel pounded me to the earth a third time. Face-first.

I held my hands out, trying to stop the pounding. Both hands snapped at the wrists. Everything seemed to break in my face. I coughed out a bunch of teeth. I think I did black out. The next thing I felt was being spun around in the air, like someone about to throw a discus, and then I *was* that discus.

I bounced off a wall and tumbled to the floor. Ethereal energy still pushed through me, but a trickle now. A cold so chill it burned as it raced through my body. The pain centered on my wrists, the knife in my side, my face.

I'm pretty sure I screamed the whole time. My wrists fit themselves together, making little popping sounds. The knife dug into me, and I tugged it out, letting it clatter to the stones underneath me.

Blood jetted out of me, my heart loping oddly at its loss, beating in a lurching kind of rhythm. I pulled more ghost. The freezing chill burned through my body, like ice pushed along my veins. My heart beat more regular. More blood was made. I kept pulling more, until the wound closed. Until my cheekbones formed back together. Until my teeth grew back. I pulled more and more, harder and harder, until I felt Azir pop, like a balloon ...

All kinds of memories flew through me. Azir, running away. Azir and his big friend. Later on, the thin man. All of them fleeing, at times. Laugh-

ing, at others. The three of them facing vampires. Wights. Werewolves. Creatures of all kinds.

I learned a little history of the Key. There was a brief memory of Azir reading script from an almost-ruined parchment, in a dark cave. It had been created by Solomon. He had trapped the demons in the stone, and passed the Key on to the first keeper when he died.

Azazel showed up in Azir's memories often. The demon usually popped in at the end of one memory, before it transitioned to another time, another place. Each time Azazel appeared, there had been a fight, people had died. Usually in messy ways, screaming.

Hundreds of those memories flickered through me, faster and faster, like a movie reel spinning out of control.

Azir had been on the run a long time. People died around him, all the time. At one point there had been more than Azir, Sameer, and Zahir. There had been dozens. They had traveled deserts, like a caravan. Staying in the sunlight, stopping at an oasis, and occasionally a town.

Fewer people appeared, memory by memory. As if time had picked them off. The caravan grew smaller, became less. Clothes got more ragged. People grew older. Dirtier. Wrapped in bandages. Then were gone.

And then, just a few days ago, a last memory of Azir, Sameer, and Zahir. All standing on top of the mountain, looking down at the monastery. The dirty white jeep parked behind them, running, a steady chug-chug-chug.

"Why here?" Sameer asked.

Azir shook his head. The Key, heavy on his chest, tugging down on his neck. "I do not know. I only understand it pulls me this way."

"I do not like this," Sameer said. "It rarely tells you anything. There was the cave, the scripts, that one time."

"And that ended well," the thin man with the ponytail, Zahir, said, rolling his eyes.

They spoke Arabic. Though I wasn't sure how I knew that. Or understood them …

There was some regret then that I felt from Azir's ghost. Understanding that he had seen the changes in Zahir, over time. The growing despair. Zahir had become more and more quiet, over the years. Withdrawn.

Until he had given up, and the rakshasa had taken him.

Then the memory went on …

"It has been a long journey," Azir answered, with a sigh. "Maybe, maybe it is time for another."

"Well," Sameer said, simply. Then repeated himself, as if he wanted to have more to say, but didn't. "Well …"

"I know," Azir said.

There was a warble of birds in the air. Wings fluttered past them. The monastery glowed in the morning sun as the shadows of the mountain around it pulled back, during the rise of the sun.

"Bah," Sameer finally said, with a grin. "What else would we have done?"

"I would have eaten less of your cooking," Azir said, with a grin.

Zahir remained quiet. But Azir and the big man laughed, at an old joke made many times. One of the many things that had tied them together, until now. Through all the running, the fighting, through all the deaths.

It was likely there would be three more soon. And they all knew it. Or at least, two of them did.

"I am still sad," Azir said.

"It is life," Sameer said. "To be sad, if this is the end, is fitting. It means we have learned. We grew. So now we look back. We regret. We wish. And we hope."

The big man shrugged. "It is life," he repeated.

Azir turned around, looking up the hill. He felt something there, something coming toward them. Not the presence of the demon, but something else.

Something new.

His fingers clutched the Key, and he wished. And hoped. And most of all, regretted …

The ghost popped. Disappeared. Taking his energy with him.

Azazel slammed me against the floor one more time, then let me go. Everything inside me ached, and what didn't ache was a hot, burning pain.

I cried out and continued to crawl. Trying to get away. The last wisps of the ethereal energy sank into my skin and drifted through the body. I didn't feel the cooling sensation as much as a deep fatigue, a numbing.

I got to the top of the rubble and collapsed. I couldn't move any farther. I was too tired. Too exhausted. In way, way too much pain, so much pain my body had shut me down, shut it all down.

Footsteps crunched on gravel, each step digging into the rubble as Azazel climbed up to me. The stupid finches kept chirping somewhere. The demon spoke, and when he did, he sounded excited. "This is just day one, Grimm. And I can't help but wonder where this all ends."

The memories of Azir flew through me again. The hundreds of times Azazel had trapped him. The times he had to fight and run. The times he had to watch people die and flee. All of them ending the same way, with Azir running. Sometimes with others, sometimes alone, and all of it had ended here.

With his body broken, crushed. A creature digging into his leg. The man dying. Dead. And then tossed aside like garbage.

The gravel shifted. Azazel knelt next to me. The demon waited patiently. After an hour, or a minute, hell, I had no idea, maybe a fucking week, I opened my eyes.

Azazel had his grin back. Pearly white teeth shining in the bright light of day. He squatted in front of me, his shirt and jacket clean and whole, as if he had just bought it off the rack. The demon pulled a handkerchief out of his suit pocket, and patted his forehead here and there. "It's a long way to any place out here, Grimm," he said.

I let out a deep breath. That was all I had left. I felt like I was dead. I should have been dead, like Suzy. Like Jason. Like all of Recon Team Four.

For some reason, I kept on living when others died. It was why I had left my hometown, back in Grafton. Why I had joined the army, and stayed overseas. It was why I was here now. And it was why I would keep going.

"Get a head start," the demon told me, from my side. "Round two, tomorrow, you know."

I didn't want to, but I looked. The blue sky overhead, the white crests of the Hindu Kush perched on top of the tall blue stone of the mountains. White clouds drifting in front of a bright yellow sun. A beautiful day, in any life but mine, and my team's.

There was a *tut-tut* sound. As if Azazel was disappointed. The demon leaned close enough that his breath was hot against my cheek. It stank like rotten meat. He placed a hand lovingly on my back. Like he was a buddy.

"All you have to do," he whispered, "is hand it over."

Then he was gone. Just like that.

I lay there for a long time. Teetering on the edge of giving up and going on. Birds called out, snowfinchs or not, who cared? Pebbles clicked against pebbles as four-legged animals crept back from wherever they had hid. Creatures that had no idea about monsters hunting some Key, demons playing a game, or the fate of the world resting in a tiny flat stone.

Then a quick dragging sound. Like jeans, pulled briefly along the ground. A groan. An exhale, after a hard exertion. I found myself standing, not fully conscious of how I had gotten that way. I held the shotgun in one hand. And I faced west, where the sun would descend into its dark grave, leaving the world bathed in blackness. At least for a time.

Azir had trusted someone else. That person had betrayed him, in the end. Zahir had seen all his friends die. Maybe family. And as their numbers dwindled, Zahir had made a choice. He hadn't wanted to be next.

Azir had trusted those around him. The same friends and family. I would not make the same mistake he had. I would not cost those I loved their lives. I would not force my friends to have to make the same choice Zahir had.

I had witnessed, both in his memories and here, in the Hindu Kush, what happened when you stayed close to people you cared about. I had run from the same thing, back in Grafton. Another mistake I promised never to make again.

Then I took a step. Shaky, my foot dragging along the rocky ground, until I carefully placed it on the sliding stones. Put a little weight on it.

Azazel had made a mistake leaving me alive. Wanting me to play his silly game. I had run from demons before, and I could run from this one until I figured out what to do next.

I seemed somehow to remain standing, even as my friends died. It was a curse, but I would use it. I would keep living, until I put a stop to whatever Azazel wanted. That I promised myself.

I looked up the hill. Past the shattered walls, to the mound of rubble lying against the hillside, rubble that used to be a monastery. I made a promise to the people there, too.

Azazel would be back. The demon had told me so. I needed to be gone before then. Demons had been chasing this stone for a long time. That would end with me, someday. All I had to do was stay alive, stay on the move, until I could find a way to make Azazel feel the type of regret people feel when they are faced with both barrels of their bad choices.

I took another breath, a deeper one. And then another step. You could almost call it walking, though I held my hands out, like a man keeping his balance on a high wire.

The shotgun lay before me, on the ground. I bent down to pick it up, even though it was empty. The world swam around me as I did, and I paused again. Taking a deep breath, and letting my sense of balance come back to me.

The wind picked up, the chill morning air coming down from the Hindu Kush fluttering loose pieces of clothing around me. My jacket, a little torn, a little ragged, but still whole. Birds chirped in the air, tiny warbling cries greeting the morning. No matter what had happened to me, here, to my friends, it was just another day for them.

I dug deep inside me, for a hard, granitelike resolve. Something unbreakable that would not yield in the years to come. Until this was finished, between the demon and me.

My hand tightened around the stock of the shotgun. My eyes focused on my shadow before me, long along the ground. I took one more step.

Then another.

Enjoy *Recon Team Four* and want a more of Grimm?

The next in the series, *City of the Dead,* is ready and waiting for you at your favorite book seller of choice.

After that, come visit chrisjcranford.com and be a part of the Grimm Universe. Discover all the worlds I'm building. Or just reach out and say hello.

While you're waiting for the book to arrive, flip to the next page for the first chapter of *City of the Dead*.

I'm excited to have you along this ride.

CITY OF THE DEAD

It was a new day. Never mind that we had left Grafton only that morning. That most of us were exhausted from the battle, the night before. It was new, because we were all alive. Together. *Free*.

We were at a gas station. It was early in the drive, but we needed a break. Walk around a minute, grab something quick to eat.

The sky above was an empty, pale blue. It was marred only by faint, dark smudges of smoke that rose above the hills north of us. The sun drifted its way westward, a yellow orb radiating little warmth. We were still in the mountains, and the air carried a chill only late autumn could bring. Not many hours of daylight were left, and when night fell it would bring the icy cold promise of the coming winter.

I stood, gas nozzle in hand, staring at the empty skies above me, the cold hills we descended out of. I took a deep breath, inhaling the strong smell of manure from the gently sloped land around the station. Farm animals, in the fields around us.

The mountainside behind us took on the shape of a slumbering giant tucked under a blanket of browning grass, dotted with black specks of cows. Here and there I could see the giant's features, the slumbering head, tilted to one side. The crook of an elbow. The round shape of a knee ...

I tried to ignore the dark columnlike clouds above the giant in the north. The trails of smoke lifting high over Grafton. The homes there must still be burning, and tall ashlike fingers stretched into the skies, one last grasp of a town no longer alive.

No longer anything.

Just a few hours ago I had killed Raphael. Nick and Johnny and I had buried Father Ben. Sarah and Jen had hugged and cried. Nick and I had talked, apologized, and forgiven each other.

Then we had driven out of town.

I put the handle into the tank and squeezed it, felt the hard pump of gas kick through the hose, followed by the rippling feel of gasoline pulse into the tank. The smell of gasoline drifted from out of the tank, which oddly enough, I liked.

Nick and Johnny were in the store, seeing what food they could scrounge up with what little cash we had. Sarah had gone with them, quiet and withdrawn but staying by Nick as much as she could. Something she had never done when we were kids. Which was just one of the changes in her.

They had used science and dark magic back in Grafton to turn Sarah's blood into a drug. Any vampire who bit her would be able to control other vampires, in much the same way as a curse could control me.

The same process that had changed her blood had also turned her into some kind of supernatural time bomb. Sarah's clock was ticking. I didn't know how much time we – *she* – had left. And I had destroyed the place that could have reset her clock to zero.

No one had mentioned that problem yet, but in the rearview mirror I had seen her in the backseat, jaw set tight, wincing at every loud noise. We needed to find a fix. A cure. The sooner, the better.

I had broken what might have fixed her, back in Grafton. I didn't know what I had done, back at the factory. I was just trying to rescue Jen. But in the middle of a fight, as I was pulling ghosts, an explosion had burst out of me. A wave of force that had cracked the concrete floors of the factory, destroying the sigils and the equipment the doctor had used to create Sarah and the drug controlling the vampires.

Before that moment, I was just a guy who could see ghosts, and who could tap into the ethereal plane through each spirit, using the energy to make myself faster, stronger. I had never exploded anything before. Well, not without a lot of C-4.

Things had changed for me in Grafton. Armor had grown out of my skin. I had healed Jen. I had met my mother. I had killed Raphael, one of the most vicious monsters I had ever faced.

Danny had been a large part of that victory over Raphael. Even though his ghost was long gone, I still felt his spirit like the echo of a song that stayed in your head. His ghost had appeared and shown how to forgive myself, and I had used what Danny had given me to kill Raphael and rescue my friends.

I had missed the sleight of hand, though. The real reason I was in Grafton. By the time I had realized that everything happening had been to distract me, it was too late. Like a three-cup game, I had been so focused on following the ball I hadn't seen the trick.

I looked to the south and felt the pull of the Key. Azazel still had it, was drifting away from us even now. It would be hard to catch him, and although I didn't regret my choices, in Grafton, it was hard for me to just let Azazel go. The demon liked his games, and though I felt like I was more of a match for him now than I had been, I was tired of playing.

But all of that was before.

Now was for after.

"Hey." Jen leaned out of the passenger's side of the car and smiled at me. One of her hands drew circles on the outside of the car door, and her long blond hair wisped a bit in the slight breeze.

I could get used to that smile, but I wouldn't.

"Hey." I grinned back at her. Amazed at being with her, again.

"What'cha thinking?" she asked.

I motioned north. "It's hard to believe we can still see the smoke."

Jen twisted a little in the window to look, one hand covering her eyes. The smoke had hung behind us while we were driving, always present in the rearview mirror, tiny columns of darkness that twisted and turned and thinned out over the distance like slender, smoky fingers of a beckoning hand.

A shadow hanging behind us, the smoldering flames over our past, not quite ready to dissolve away.

"It's hard to believe that was the town we grew up in," Jen said.

"So much happened there," I said. "And now it's all gone."

The town was dead. And along with it, people who had taken care of me. Whom I had cared about. Miss Tammie. Parker, Danny. Even Father Ben, Greg.

All the deaths didn't seem worth what I had figured out about myself. I had learned I couldn't protect those I cared about by running. I learned that I needed to be there, for them. I just couldn't protect them all.

It didn't seem fair. And I had killed the person responsible. But I hadn't killed Azazel. And now I had lost the Key. I looked south again, feeling its pull.

Jen got out of the car. Shut the door and leaned against me a moment. Her body was warm against mine. Her scent of honeysuckle and fresh rain overpowered everything. I took a breath and, as always, felt a little better.

She nuzzled her face into the hollow of my throat and ran her hand up and down my arm. My skin tingled in response, like I had stuck my finger into a light socket. It was electric.

"I can't figure out whether it's you doing that," I said. "Or it's you *doing that*."

She waggled her eyebrows against my cheek. I laughed. Jen was a storm witch, something I didn't know until yesterday. It was hard to believe the woman I had come to Grafton to rescue was the same woman who had been throwing lightning bolts like she was striking out a side.

But it wasn't hard to believe she was the same girl I had fallen in love with. Back when we were kids, eating cereal on the couch, watching Saturday morning reruns. Back when she could smile at me, and I felt a little taller.

"Have we figured out where we're going?" Jen asked.

I shook my head. We were headed south for now, it being the fastest way out of Grafton. But also because of the pull of the Key. It still called to me, even though Azazel had it.

The demon had warned me off from following him. I had buried the Key while in Grafton, and Nick had found it and given it to Azazel in exchange for Sarah, after thinking I had been killed. Not that I faulted Nick. I hadn't been the best Keeper, just the latest one, and I would make the same trade if had meant saving Jen.

He had left one last message to me. I could protect my friends, or I could come after the Key, but I couldn't do both. But I had learned a valuable lesson in Grafton. Protecting my friends wasn't all on me. Life sucked sometimes, and I needed to take responsibility not only for the lives of my friends, but for their deaths as well. Not everyone always made it, and I would always try, but I would no longer run from my failures.

Azazel wanted me twisting in the wind, worried about my friends, and worried what would happen if the demon released his brothers and sisters. The person I had been a few days ago would have been terrified. The new me had learned a lesson, to lean on my friends' strengths, to include them in a burden shared. It wouldn't just be me coming after Azazel. It would be me and Jen and Nick and Sarah and Johnny.

"You got serious quick," Jen said.

I didn't answer. She knew I wasn't one for a lot of words. Especially when the words mattered. It felt good to be with her, to be with my friends, to be with people who counted on me and believed in me and in turn wanted me to believe in them.

But it also felt strange. The dynamic was something I needed to get used to. I had been alone for a long time, and I hadn't been a great friend before then. I was trying to learn how to be one now.

I looked over to the gas station. Jen's sister was in the station with Nick and Johnny. The magic she carried would kill her, if we didn't get her help. As much as I wanted to beat Azazel at his game, my friends would come first. I had learned that lesson now.

Jen sensed what I was feeling. Kissed me lightly on the cheekbone and whispered in my ear, "Be right back."

She was never going to press. Jen was just always going to be there. I was having trouble getting used to that kind of acceptance, of having someone always in my corner. Maybe a little irrationally, I feared losing it.

She strode toward the gas station, legs and curves and athletic grace. The door to the store opened. Jen walked in as Nick and Johnny walked out. The two guys were arguing which candy bar was better, and the argument got louder as they came near. There was a serious discussion about whether a peanut butter cup could be allowed into a candy bar debate.

"What do you think, Grimm?" Johnny asked.

The nozzle for the gas pump kicked off, and I pulled it out of the tank and hung the handle on the pump. I stared at them both. "Peanut butter cups have to be allowed."

"Told you." Nick grinned.

"Then you can't have a debate," Johnny said. "Nothing beats a peanut butter cup."

"Exactly," I agreed.

"No one lets airplanes get into a fastest car discussion," Johnny said.

Nick made a motion that meant, *see what I'm dealing with?*

"That's because planes aren't cars," I said.

"Then peanut butter cups aren't candy bars," Johnny argued. "Right?"

"I think I'd say that once you fly somewhere in a plane, you realize it's the peanut butter cup of how to travel." I patted the roof of my car a few times to let her know no hard feelings. "No matter how fast the car."

"But they're not a candy *bar*," Johnny said. "Emphasis on the square shape."

I raised my eyebrows. "It's candy, though. So for the purpose of this discussion, I'm firmly in the peanut-butter-cup camp."

Johnny rolled his eyes.

"Guess what?" Nick handed me a Coke and some kind of clawlike pastry, the kind with white icing and thick cinnamon filling. "Those witches we saved? They were here yesterday."

I remembered Tabitha at the factory. She had been an earth witch of some power. She had left with her daughter and the rest of the witches after I had freed them.

"Nick thinks we should find them," Johnny added.

"It's not a bad idea," Nick said. He looked over at the front of the gas station. In the window we could all see Jen talking to Sarah. "They might know something that could help."

I looked over at Jen and Sarah, at Sarah's pinched, withdrawn face. At Jen's worry. At Nick, earnestly looking at me.

Just a few days ago Nick had punched me. And up until this morning, he hadn't trusted me. And I understood why. Up until a few days ago, I had let all of my friends down. Maybe Nick, most of all. And even though it was Nick's fault that the demon had the Key, I understood his reasons there as well. I told him I would have done the same, and I would have.

Nick and I had forgiven each other. Though he seemed tentative around me. Nervous maybe, stuck somewhere between the hard man he was now, a man who walked shadows, and the younger kid brother he had used to be.

Or maybe he was just worried about Sarah. The girl he had grown up with a crush on. Whom he had stayed in Grafton for, even though she – at the time – had wanted nothing more than his friendship.

Raphael, the vampire I had killed, had created a mind-controlling drug, one vampires were massively addicted to. Though he needed some kind of control for the drug, and had made that with Sarah. She had gone through some kind of ritual that had turned her blood into the power by which Raphael could control any of the vampires that drank his drug.

Sarah was paler now than earlier today. Her eyes were constantly pinched. Jen had told me Sarah had thrown up that morning at the hotel, and she was having trouble eating since.

We would have to find her help soon. The witches were as good a bet as anyone.

"Sure, man," I said. "Let's look for them."

Nick whooped loud enough that both Jen and Sarah looked at him from inside the station.

Johnny winked at me. I took a bite of pastry, tasting the sweet icing and the cinnamon, and waited for the girls to come back out. When they did, they had a variety of sugary snacks and a couple of bottles of fancy water, the colored kind with electrolytes. Jen was talking Sarah into drinking some.

Sarah's skin was even paler than a few hours ago. Little black lines, like thin veins, appeared and disappeared under the surface of her skin. She had bought a baseball cap in the store, and had it pulled snug over her head. The rim laid a shadow across her eyes.

I watched Sarah force down a swig of the water and grimace at the taste. "You okay?"

She nodded. We had been close once. She had been like a little sister. I remembered a girl who loved teasing Jen and me whenever we were snuggled together on the couch. Now, out of all my friends, Sarah and I had grown the most apart. Or at least there seemed to be a larger gulf between us than before.

It hurt me, back when I had first come to Grafton. I had seen Sarah, and she had told me to save her sister and go. Like Sarah believed she herself wasn't worth saving.

It hurt deeper at the time, because I had come into town with just that intention. My full plan was to rescue Jen and run. It still hurt now, even though I believed I had changed. At least, I wanted to change.

"Nick mentioned the group of witches we rescued from the factory," I told her. "We're going to find them and see if they can help."

"Okay," Sarah said, simply. She eased past me to get into the car. Nick climbed in after her, and Johnny slapped me on the shoulder before getting in.

I took another bite of the pastry and walked around to the other side of the Camaro and got in. I hoped somehow we could help Sarah. Or what happened to her, that would be all on me.

Johnny started up the candy bar debate again, this time trying to get Jen on his side, talking about square shapes versus round ones. Listening, as I fired up the car, I thought it sounded as if he fought an uphill battle. It was four to one against. But he still argued on.

I grinned. There was a sense of the old us, the old times, of the Wolverines, with Johnny. With just the argument about a candy bar. Or a peanut butter cup. It was a feeling I'd missed, and it was nice to be reminded that it was the five of us versus the world.

I drove the Camaro out onto the road. The car accelerated quickly and bounced over a rough spot where the on-ramp met the interstate. Sarah winced, hard, and grabbed for Nick's hand.

Farther back behind Sarah, in the rearview mirror, were the faint smudges of smoke over Grafton. Trailing over the mountains. A past we all were trying to leave behind.

I focused forward. South. Where the Key still pulled at me. Toward Azazel, and whatever game he wanted to play.

My foot pushed harder on the gas. The Camaro surged forward. Jen gave me a questioning look, which I shrugged off.

Sarah. The Key. Maybe it was the life I had lived up until now, but I had a feeling those two were going to collide. It was a premonition I could not shake, no matter that it made no sense.

ABOUT THE AUTHOR

When Chris isn't trying to figure out how to write a bio, he spends time contemplating the fate of the universe. Probably while walking into a door jamb. He's accepted that the two go hand-in-hand.

He currently resides in Florida, though he has some Magellan in him, and loves to wander.

It is his dream to write stories that – through their telling – influence others to live a little better. Stand a little taller. Smile a little wider. Hold someone a little longer. Fiction should be the dream real life aspires to be.

Dogs are his buddies. Football is his hobby. Books are his passion.

Find out more about Chris here:

www.chrisjcranford.com

facebook.com/chrisjcranford

 x.com/chrisjcranford

 instagram.com/chrisjcranford

9 781961 138384